Possessed Doll

Alexis Jones

Published by Alexis Jones, 2024.

This is a work of fiction. Similarities to real people, places, or events are entirely coincidental.

POSSESSED DOLL

First edition. October 21, 2024.

Copyright © 2024 Alexis Jones.

ISBN: 979-8224482672

Written by Alexis Jones.

Dedication

The Northshore Academy of Martial Arts Dojo crew. You were there when I was younger and I don't know if I would be at the place I'm at now. You guys have been my rock in the past and I love the dojo. Thank you for being there for me when I was younger and being there for me now.

Alexandru Jociva, Thank you for being a great sensei and always believing in me. If it weren't for you, I don't know if this would be possible. You have helped me through so much and continue to be there for me.

Matthew Hibbeler, Thank you for being there when I need you. We may have our ups and downs, but there is always something between us that is unbreakable. These past few years have been wonderful and I love being with you. Thank you for helping me with this book, and many more to come. There is always going to be us, and I appreciate everything you have done. I love you so much and I don't know where I would be without you.

Chapter 1

The rain beat down in steady sheets, turning the city streets into rivers of reflected neon light. Lena gripped the steering wheel of her old sedan, the rhythmic thump of the windshield wipers barely keeping up with the storm's relentless pace. Her breath fogged the glass as she squinted through the mist, searching for the small, out-of-the-way antique shop she'd read about online.

"'Lasting Impressions'... where are you?" she muttered, scanning the block. She'd passed this road at least three times but somehow kept missing it.

Just as she was about to turn around again, a small, dimly lit sign flickered on a narrow side street—*Lasting Impressions Antiques*. The sign swayed in the wind, the worn lettering barely visible beneath the grime of countless seasons. Lena frowned. From what she'd read, the place was a treasure trove of rare finds, but it didn't look like much from the outside.

"Well, this better be worth it," she said to herself as she parked the car. She pulled up her hood and dashed through the rain toward the shop, the cold wind cutting through her jacket like knives.

The door creaked as she pushed it open, and a small brass bell above it jingled weakly, the sound almost swallowed by the howling wind. Inside, the air was stale, tinged with the smell of old wood and dust. The shop was dimly lit by a few flickering candles and a series of old-fashioned lamps, casting long shadows over the cluttered shelves and glass cases. It felt like stepping into another time, a forgotten era where every object had a story to tell—if you dared to listen. Rows of ancient furniture, tarnished silverware, and faded paintings crowded the space, while old clocks ticked softly from every corner. Each one seemed to be counting down to something, though Lena couldn't quite place what. The eerie atmosphere clung to her like the dampness from the rain. She walked deeper into the shop, her eyes darting from object to object. A gilded mirror reflected her pale, rain-streaked face as she passed, making her shiver. Lena had always liked old things. They had history, a past. And this year, she wanted something special for Marie's birthday—something unique that would make her smile, something unlike the usual trinkets or gifts. But so far, nothing called to her. Then she saw it. It was tucked away in the far corner of the shop, almost hidden behind a towering wooden cabinet. A doll, just sitting there, staring back at her from the shadows. The candlelight flickered, casting strange, shifting shadows across its face. Lena hesitated. It wasn't like any doll she'd seen before—this one was unsettling. Its porcelain skin was pale, cracked in places as though it had endured more than a century of silent existence. Dark, curly hair framed its face, and its eyes—those cold, glassy eyes—seemed to follow her every move. The doll wore a lace dress, yellowed with age, and a small embroidered heart over its chest. Its tiny, delicate hands rested in its lap, but something about its stillness unnerved Lena. She glanced around the shop, wondering if anyone else had noticed the eerie doll, but the place seemed deserted. The only sound was the ticking of the clocks and the distant rumble of thunder from the storm outside. She stepped closer, drawn to the doll despite her discomfort. Her fingers hovered over its face, hesitating. The porcelain looked like it would be ice-cold to the touch.

"Beautiful, isn't it?" a voice rasped from behind her.

Lena jumped, spinning around to face the source of the voice. An old man stood behind the counter, his face as worn and craggy as the items that filled the shop. His eyes, dark and sunken, glinted with something Lena couldn't quite place—something like amusement, or maybe warning.

"Uh, yeah. I guess," Lena said, clearing her throat. "It's... different."

The old man smiled, revealing a row of yellowed teeth. "Oh, it's more than different, dear. That one's special."

"Special?" Lena echoed, raising an eyebrow. She turned back to the doll, its blank face giving nothing away.

The shopkeeper stepped forward, his footsteps barely making a sound on the worn floorboards. "That doll has been here a long time. Longer than you might think. It's seen many things. Belonged to many people."

Lena frowned, feeling a slight chill crawl up her spine. "What do you mean by that?"

He gave her a long, appraising look before answering, his voice low. "Some say it's cursed. But then again, people always like to make stories out of things they don't understand, don't they?"

"Cursed?" Lena couldn't help but laugh, though the sound came out a little strained. "That's a bit much, don't you think?"

The shopkeeper didn't laugh. He only stared at her, the weight of his gaze heavy. "You don't believe me. That's fine. Most don't, at first. But I'll tell you this—every person who's taken that doll home... something bad has happened."

Lena felt her stomach tighten, but she shook her head, dismissing the man's words as part of a sales tactic. She was a skeptic at heart, never one to fall for superstitions or ghost stories. Besides, Marie loved weird, quirky things. This doll would be perfect for her collection.

"How much?" she asked, cutting through the tension.

The old man's eyes narrowed slightly, as if he were measuring her decision. After a long pause, he said, "For you, fifty."

"Fifty? For an old doll?" Lena said, raising an eyebrow.

He shrugged. "It's your choice. But I'd advise you to be careful with it. Don't say I didn't warn you."

Lena hesitated only for a moment longer before pulling out her wallet. A strange sense of unease settled in her chest, but she ignored it, chalking it up to the gloomy weather and the man's creepy demeanor. She handed him the money and carefully wrapped the doll in a blanket the shopkeeper offered her. As she did, she couldn't help but feel that the doll's glassy eyes were still watching her, even through the thick fabric.

"Thanks," she muttered, eager to leave the shop's oppressive atmosphere.

The old man said nothing as she left, his eyes following her every step. As the door creaked shut behind her, the bell's weak jingle was swallowed by the sound of the storm raging outside. Lena hurried to her car, the doll clutched tightly under her arm. She placed it gently in the backseat before sliding into the driver's seat. As she drove away, she glanced in the rearview mirror and saw the doll's face peeking out from beneath the blanket. Its eyes glistened in the dim light of the street lamps, and for a fleeting moment, Lena could have sworn it had moved slightly. She blinked and shook her head.

"Just my imagination," she whispered, turning her focus back to the road.

But deep down, she couldn't shake the feeling that something—someone—was watching her.

Chapter 2

The rain had finally let up by the time Lena got home, but the air was still thick with humidity, and the night seemed unnaturally quiet. She stepped out of the car, cradling the doll in her arms, and glanced at her house—a modest two-story cottage at the edge of town, nestled among a grove of towering oak trees. The trees swayed gently in the breeze, their branches creaking like old bones. Lena shook off the chill creeping up her spine and hurried up the porch steps. She unlocked the door and slipped inside, the warmth of the house welcoming her after the damp, stormy night. As she set her keys on the side table, Luna, her black cat, darted across the room, her green eyes wide and her fur bristling.

"Hey, Luna, it's just me," Lena said, trying to soothe the cat. But Luna remained on edge, her eyes fixed on the doll still wrapped in the blanket.

Lena glanced down at the doll, an uneasy feeling creeping back into her chest. "You don't like it either, huh?" she muttered.

She unwrapped the doll carefully, setting it on the dining table to get a better look. The porcelain face, now illuminated by the soft overhead light, looked more fragile than it had in the dimly lit antique shop. But what unsettled Lena the most were its eyes. They gleamed with a strange light, reflecting the house's dim glow almost too well.

"Marie's gonna love you," Lena whispered, though the words felt hollow in her mouth.

The clock on the wall chimed softly, breaking the silence. It was late, and Lena felt the weight of exhaustion from the long day. She decided to leave the doll on the table and head upstairs to get some sleep. As she turned off the lights, she cast one last glance at the doll, sitting perfectly still in the darkened room. But in the dim light, for just a split second, she thought she saw the doll's head turn ever so slightly, its glassy eyes catching the moonlight. Lena blinked, shaking her head. "I'm seeing things," she muttered to herself, quickly heading up the stairs. She brushed her teeth and changed into her pajamas, trying to push the unsettling thought out of her mind. It had been a long day, and she was just tired. That's all it was. But that night, her sleep was fitful. She tossed and turned beneath the covers, her dreams filled with shadowy figures and whispered voices. The air felt heavy in her dream, like something unseen was pressing down on her. And somewhere in the darkness, she could see a pair of glassy, unblinking eyes watching her. She woke up with a start, her heart racing, cold sweat trickling down her neck. For a moment, she lay still, listening to the silence of the house, her breath shallow. Then, slowly, she turned her head toward the doorway of her bedroom. Her heart leaped into her throat.

The doll was sitting on the floor by the door, propped up against the wall, its head tilted at an odd angle as if it were watching her. Lena blinked, her mind racing. Had she brought the doll upstairs last night? No. She distinctly remembered leaving it downstairs on the table. But there it was, its lifeless eyes staring straight at her. For a long moment, she just stared at the doll, her pulse quickening. Then, telling herself it was some kind of mistake, she threw back the covers and got out of bed. As she approached the doll, every instinct in her body told her to stay away from it, but she pushed the feeling aside. This was ridiculous. It was just a doll. Nothing more. She picked it up, her hands trembling slightly as she did. The porcelain was cold to the touch, sending a chill up her arms. Without a second thought, she carried it back downstairs and set it on the table where she'd left it the night before.

"I must have moved it," she said aloud, trying to reassure herself. "I was probably half-asleep and didn't even realize."

But even as she said it, she knew it wasn't true. That morning, the sun streamed through the windows, casting warm, golden light across the house. The brightness of the day made last night's strange events feel distant, like a bad dream. Lena busied herself with work, trying to shake off the lingering unease. She worked from home as a freelance designer, and there were deadlines to meet, clients to respond to. The normalcy of it all helped her forget the strangeness of the night. Still, every now and then, she would catch herself glancing toward the doll on the table, half-expecting it to move again. But it didn't. It just sat there, unmoving, as all dolls should. By mid-afternoon, Lena was feeling a bit more settled. Maybe she had just been overtired last night. It wouldn't be the first time she'd had weird dreams after a long day. Marie was coming over for dinner, and Lena was eager to give her the doll. She set the table, making sure everything was perfect for her sister's visit. As she did, she heard a soft creaking sound behind her. Lena froze. Slowly, she turned toward the sound, her heart beating fast. The doll was sitting in a different position. She had left it upright, with its hands neatly folded in its lap. But now, one of its arms was stretched out toward the edge of the table, as if it had reached for something. Lena's mouth went dry. She hadn't touched it. She knew she hadn't.

"Stop it," she whispered to herself, her voice trembling. "It's just your imagination."

She reached out to adjust the doll back into its original position, but as her fingers brushed its cold porcelain hand, a soft, barely audible sound escaped the doll's mouth. A faint giggle. Lena jerked her hand back, stumbling away from the table, her heart pounding in her chest. She stared at the doll, her breath coming in shallow gasps. Had it just... laughed?

"No," she whispered, shaking her head. "No, that's not possible."

She backed away, her pulse racing, and grabbed her phone, dialing Marie's number with trembling fingers.

"Hey, sis! What's up?" Marie's cheerful voice came through the line, but Lena could barely focus.

"I—uh, I think you should come over early," Lena stammered, her eyes never leaving the doll. "I've got something for you."

"Sure! I can be there in half an hour," Marie replied, sensing the urgency in Lena's voice. "You okay?"

"I'm fine," Lena lied. "Just... hurry."

She hung up and paced the room, glancing nervously at the doll every few seconds. Her rational mind was fighting against the rising panic, telling her that there was a logical explanation for all of this. Maybe it was some kind of prank. Maybe the doll had some sort of mechanical feature she didn't know about. But no matter how hard she tried to explain it away, that small, faint giggle echoed in her mind, growing louder and louder with each passing minute. By the time Marie arrived, Lena was a nervous wreck. She rushed to the door and let her sister in, barely giving her a chance to take off her coat before leading her into the dining room.

"Okay, you've got to see this," Lena said, her voice shaking as she gestured to the doll.

Marie blinked, confused. "Uh, it's a doll. A really creepy doll, but... what am I supposed to be looking at?"

"It—it moved, Marie. It's been moving on its own," Lena said, her words tumbling out in a frantic rush.

Marie laughed, clearly thinking Lena was joking. "You've been working too hard, sis. Dolls don't just move on their own."

"I'm not making this up!" Lena snapped, her frustration mixing with fear. "I put it on the table last night, and this morning, it was upstairs in my room. Then just now, it... it laughed."

Marie's smile faltered, seeing how serious Lena was. "Okay, okay. Show me what it does."

Lena took a deep breath and turned toward the doll, but it remained perfectly still, its hands neatly folded in its lap, just as it had been when Marie walked in. It looked innocent, lifeless. Just a regular old doll.

"Come on, Lena," Marie said gently. "It's just a doll. Maybe you're stressed out and imagining things."

Lena stared at it, her hands clenching into fists at her sides. "I know what I heard," she whispered.

Marie shrugged and walked over to the doll, picking it up and inspecting it. "Look, it's fine. See? No mechanical parts, nothing weird about it. You're just overthinking things."

But as Marie held the doll in her arms, Lena couldn't shake the feeling that those glassy eyes were staring straight at her, mocking her. That night, the doll was back in Lena's dreams. Only this time, the doll wasn't watching her from a distance. It was standing at the foot of her bed, its tiny porcelain hand resting on her ankle. And the last thing she heard before waking up, drenched in sweat, was the sound of that faint, sinister giggle.

Chapter 3

The next morning, Lena awoke to the sound of birds chirping outside her window. The early morning light filtered through the curtains, casting soft, golden rays across the room. For a brief moment, everything felt normal. But then, the events of the previous night came flooding back—the doll, the strange giggle, the way it had moved on its own. She sat up slowly, her heart already beginning to race. Her eyes immediately darted to the corner of the room where she had placed the doll before bed. But it wasn't there. Lena's breath caught in her throat as she scanned the room, her pulse quickening. There, sitting on the chair by her desk, was the doll. Its glassy eyes were fixed on her, its porcelain face still and expressionless. She hadn't moved it. She was certain of that. She had left it by the window, far away from the desk. A cold shiver ran down her spine as she swung her legs over the side of the bed and stood up. The wooden floor creaked under her feet as she cautiously approached the doll. Its eyes seemed to follow her, even though she knew that wasn't possible. Lena picked up the doll, her hands trembling slightly. It was just a doll. A lifeless object. She had to remind herself of that. But as she held it in her hands, she couldn't shake the feeling that something wasn't right. The air around her felt thick, oppressive, as if the room had become smaller, trapping her with it. She set the doll down on the bed and backed away, her heart pounding in her chest. "I need to get rid of this thing," she muttered under her breath.

The thought had been circling in her mind for days now, but every time she considered getting rid of the doll, something stopped her. It was as if an invisible force was keeping her from acting. Maybe Marie was right. Maybe she was just overthinking things. But that didn't explain why the doll kept moving on its own—or the strange, unsettling feeling she got every time she looked at it. Shaking off the thoughts, Lena grabbed her phone and headed downstairs, deciding to focus on anything but the doll for a while. She needed to clear her mind, get some fresh air. Maybe even talk to someone about it. The kitchen smelled of coffee, the familiar scent grounding her in the present. She poured herself a cup and sat at the table, scrolling through her phone absentmindedly. But no matter how hard she tried to distract herself, her mind kept drifting back to the doll. What if there really was something wrong with it? What if the shopkeeper's warning hadn't just been some silly story? Lena couldn't shake the image of his sunken eyes and the strange tone in his voice when he'd told her to be careful. A soft thud from upstairs broke her train of thought. Lena froze, her hand tightening around the mug. It sounded like something had fallen—something heavy. Her heart skipped a beat as she listened, the house suddenly feeling too big, too quiet. Another thud. This time louder. Lena stood up, her pulse racing. She put the mug down on the counter, trying to calm the rising panic in her chest. She walked to the bottom of the stairs, craning her neck to listen. The thudding continued—slow, deliberate, as if something was moving across the floor. Lena's stomach twisted in knots. She knew what was making the sound, even though she didn't want to admit it. The doll. Her hands trembled as she gripped the railing, her feet frozen to the spot. She didn't want to go upstairs. She didn't want to see what was happening. But she had to. She couldn't just ignore it. Taking a deep breath, Lena slowly climbed the stairs, each step feeling heavier than the last. The thudding had stopped, replaced by an eerie silence that made the hairs on the back of her neck stand on end. When she reached the top of the stairs, her heart pounded in her ears. She walked toward her bedroom, the door slightly ajar. The morning light cast long shadows across the hallway, and for a moment, Lena felt like she was being watched. She pushed the door open and froze. The doll was sitting on the floor in the middle of the room, its head tilted at an unnatural angle. The arm that had been resting in its lap was now stretched out toward the door, as if it had been reaching for something. But what sent a chill down Lena's spine was the deep, jagged crack that ran down the side of its porcelain face. The crack hadn't been there before. Lena's breath came in shallow gasps as she stared at the doll. How had it moved again? And where had the crack come from?

She took a step back, her hands shaking. "This isn't happening," she whispered to herself, her voice barely audible. "It's just a doll. It's just a stupid, old doll."

But deep down, she knew that wasn't true. The air in the room felt heavy, thick with something she couldn't see but could feel. It was as if the doll was radiating a dark energy, pulling her toward it. Lena felt an overwhelming urge to get rid of it—now. Without thinking, she grabbed the doll by the arm and marched down the stairs. She didn't care where she was taking it, but she needed to get it out of her house. She couldn't bear to spend another minute with it under her roof. The front door slammed behind her as she stepped out onto the porch. The morning was still quiet, the neighborhood peaceful, but Lena felt anything but calm. She carried the doll to the backyard, where a large trash bin sat near the fence. With shaking hands, she lifted the lid and tossed the doll inside. The porcelain figure landed with a hollow thud at the bottom of the bin, its cracked face staring up at her as she slammed the lid shut. Lena took a step back, breathing heavily. It was over. The doll was gone. She could finally breathe again. But as she turned to go back inside, she heard it. A soft, faint giggle, muffled by the lid of the trash bin. Lena's blood ran cold. She stood frozen in place, her eyes wide with fear. It was the same sound she had heard the night before—the same eerie, childlike laugh. But it wasn't possible. The doll was in the bin. She had gotten rid of it. Without thinking, Lena ran back into the house, slamming the door behind her. Her heart pounded in her chest as she leaned against the door, her mind racing. She was losing it. That was the only explanation. She was tired, stressed, imagining things. But even as she tried to convince herself, a nagging thought lingered in the back of her mind. What if the doll wasn't just an ordinary antique? What if there was something far darker, far more sinister at play? Lena spent the rest of the day trying to distract herself, but every little sound in the house made her jump. The creak of the floorboards, the ticking of the clock, the hum of the refrigerator—it all seemed louder, more menacing than before. That night, she lay in bed, wide awake. Every time she closed her eyes, she saw the doll's cracked face, its cold eyes watching her.

She could still hear that giggle, faint and distant, echoing in her mind. The hours passed slowly, and sleep refused to come. Lena tossed and turned, her mind a whirlwind of fear and confusion. It wasn't until the early hours of the morning that she finally drifted off, her exhaustion overtaking her fear. But her sleep was short-lived. A loud crash jolted her awake, her heart pounding in her chest. She sat up in bed, her breath coming in ragged gasps. For a moment, she thought she had dreamt it. But then she heard it again—a loud, unmistakable thud coming from downstairs. Lena's blood turned to ice as she realized where the sound had come from. The trash bin. She forced herself out of bed, her body trembling with fear. She grabbed her phone and cautiously made her way downstairs, her heart racing. The house was dark, and the only light came from the streetlamp outside, casting long, eerie shadows across the floor. She opened the back door slowly, stepping out onto the porch. The trash bin was still there, standing silently in the corner of the yard. But something was wrong. The lid was open. Lena's heart pounded in her chest as she approached the bin, her hands shaking. She reached out and lifted the lid, her breath catching in her throat. The doll was gone.

Chapter 4

Lena stood frozen on the back porch, staring at the empty trash bin. The doll was gone. A wave of dread washed over her, cold and suffocating. Her heart raced in her chest as her mind scrambled for a logical explanation, but none came. It was impossible. She had put the doll in the bin, slammed the lid shut. No one could have taken it—it had been there only hours ago. But now, the doll was gone, and Lena's instincts screamed that something far darker was at play. She backed away from the bin, the silence of the early morning pressing in around her. The streetlights outside flickered, casting long, jagged shadows across the lawn, making everything look distorted, wrong. Lena felt the hair on the back of her neck rise, as though something unseen was watching her. She turned, hurrying back inside and locking the door behind her. Her breaths came in ragged gasps as she leaned against the door, trying to calm her racing heart. It was just a doll—a cursed, creepy doll. She wasn't crazy. It had moved on its own before, and now it was gone. But how? Where? A soft creak echoed from the living room, snapping Lena out of her thoughts. Her body tensed, every muscle on edge. The house, which had always felt like a sanctuary, now felt like a trap—an oppressive, silent cage. Lena clenched her phone in her hand, considering calling someone. Marie. The police. Anyone. But who would believe her? What would she even say? That a possessed doll had disappeared from her trash bin and was now... what? Roaming her house? Before she could make a decision, the creaking sound came again, louder this time. It was coming from upstairs. Her blood turned to ice.

"No," she whispered, shaking her head. "It can't be..."

She stood in the kitchen, rooted to the spot, her eyes darting toward the staircase. The soft creaks continued, slow and deliberate, like footsteps moving across the wooden floor above her. Someone—or something—was in her house. And deep down, Lena knew exactly what it was. Her pulse quickened as she grabbed a flashlight from the drawer. She didn't dare turn on the lights. Something about the darkness felt safer, like it would shield her from whatever horror awaited upstairs. With the flashlight in hand, Lena took a deep breath and moved toward the stairs. Each step felt like a betrayal of her instincts, her body screaming at her to run the other way, to get out of the house. But she couldn't leave without knowing what was up there. She reached the bottom of the stairs and shone the flashlight upward, the narrow beam cutting through the darkness. The air at the top of the stairs felt thicker, heavier, as though the house itself was holding its breath. The hallway stretched out in front of her, the closed doors of her bedroom and the guest room standing like silent sentinels. The creaking had stopped, replaced by an eerie stillness. Lena swallowed hard and took the first step up the stairs. The wood groaned under her weight, and the sound seemed to echo through the house, unnaturally loud in the quiet. She held her breath, half-expecting something to lunge out of the shadows at any moment. When she reached the top, she hesitated, her hand gripping the banister so tightly her knuckles turned white. The door to her bedroom was ajar, just enough for her to see the dim outline of the furniture inside. The room seemed darker than it should have been, even with the flashlight beam. Lena's heart pounded in her chest as she slowly approached the door, her breath shallow. With one trembling hand, she pushed it open wider, the hinges creaking in protest. Her flashlight beam swept across the room, and for a moment, everything looked normal. Her bed was neatly made, the curtains drawn back to reveal the faint glow of dawn on the horizon. But then, the beam of light landed on something in the far corner of the room. Lena's breath hitched in her throat. The doll was sitting on the floor, propped up against the wall, its cracked face turned toward her, its glassy eyes reflecting the light. It was the same doll she had thrown away, the same doll that had disappeared from the trash bin. But now it was back, sitting in her bedroom, watching her. A soft, hollow giggle filled the room, barely more than a whisper, but unmistakable. Lena's stomach twisted, bile rising in her throat. This wasn't happening. It couldn't be happening. Her hands shook as she stepped backward, her flashlight beam flickering in and out as though the batteries were failing. The giggling stopped, and the room fell into a tense, unnatural silence. Lena's skin prickled with the sensation of being watched, but it wasn't just the doll. It was something else, something far more sinister. She turned and bolted out of the room, her heart pounding in her chest. As she ran down the stairs, she felt the walls of the house closing in on her, suffocating her with the weight of something unseen. It wasn't just the doll—there was a presence here, something ancient and malicious. Reaching the bottom of the stairs, Lena stumbled into the kitchen, her breaths coming in ragged gasps. She grabbed her phone from the counter and dialed Marie's number, her hands trembling so badly she almost dropped the phone.

Marie answered on the second ring, her voice groggy. "Lena? It's six in the morning. What's going on?"

"I... I need you to come over," Lena stammered, her voice barely above a whisper. "Please, Marie, I—something's happening. The doll... it moved again. It's in my house."

There was a long pause on the other end of the line. "Lena, you're not serious, are you? Dolls don't just move around. You probably just—"

"I didn't move it!" Lena snapped, her voice rising with panic. "I threw it away last night. I put it in the trash, and now it's back in my room. Marie, it's real. There's something wrong with that doll."

Marie sighed, her voice softening. "Okay, okay. I'll be there as soon as I can. Just... try to calm down, okay? We'll figure this out."

Lena hung up and sank into a chair at the kitchen table, her whole body trembling. She couldn't calm down. Not with that thing in her house. As she sat there, trying to steady her breathing, a sudden thought hit her. The antique shop. She had to go back. The shopkeeper had known something about the doll—he'd warned her. Maybe he knew more, maybe he could help her get rid of it for good. Lena grabbed her car keys and headed for the door. She wasn't going to wait for Marie. The sooner she got to the shop, the sooner she could get answers. She wasn't staying in the house another minute. The drive to the antique shop was a blur, the streets eerily empty in the early morning light. Lena's mind raced with questions, but none of them had answers. She kept glancing in the rearview mirror, half-expecting to see the doll sitting in the backseat, watching her with those cold, lifeless eyes. When she finally reached the shop, it looked just as she remembered it—small, unassuming, tucked away on a quiet side street. The faded sign above the door read "Curiosities and Collectibles." The windows were dark, the shop clearly closed, but Lena didn't care. She had to get inside.

She parked the car and rushed to the door, pounding on it with both fists. "Hello? Are you there? I need to talk to you!"

There was no answer, no movement from inside the shop. Lena pressed her face against the glass, trying to peer through the darkness, but she couldn't see anything. The place looked abandoned. Her heart sank. She was about to turn away when she noticed something. The door, though locked, was slightly ajar—just enough for her to push it open. Lena hesitated for a moment, then pushed the door wider and stepped inside. The air inside the shop was stale and heavy, the scent of dust and old wood filling her nostrils. The faint light from the rising sun filtered through the windows, casting long shadows across the shelves lined with strange, forgotten objects. The shop was exactly as she remembered it, but it felt different now—darker, more oppressive. She walked slowly through the narrow aisles, her eyes scanning the shelves for anything that might explain the doll's strange behavior. There were old books, worn-down trinkets, and other creepy antiques, but nothing that seemed connected to the doll. And then she saw it. At the back of the shop, on a dusty shelf near the floor, was an old, leather-bound journal. It looked ancient, the pages yellowed with age. Something about it drew Lena's attention, and she reached for it, her hands trembling. The cover was embossed with strange symbols, ones she didn't recognize, but they looked almost like runes. She opened the journal, her eyes scanning the brittle pages. The writing was in a language she couldn't understand, but there were drawings—detailed sketches of dolls, each one more grotesque than the last. Her heart pounded as she flipped through the pages. One of the drawings stopped her cold. It was the doll. The same cracked porcelain face, the same lifeless eyes. Underneath the drawing was a single word written in bold, black ink - Malphas. Lena's blood ran cold. Whatever this thing was, it had a name. She needed to get out of there.

Chapter 5

Lena clutched the journal tightly to her chest, her pulse racing as she backed away from the shelf. The word **Malphas** echoed in her mind, an ancient name that felt both familiar and foreign, like a whispered warning she couldn't fully understand. She could almost hear the shadows in the room thickening, coiling around her like smoke. With every instinct screaming at her to flee, she turned to leave, but a sudden noise froze her in place. The sound came from the front of the shop—a loud crash, as if something heavy had fallen. Lena's heart pounded as fear gripped her.

"Hello?" she called out, her voice trembling in the stillness. "Is anyone here?"

No answer. The shop seemed more oppressive than ever, the dim light filtering through the dusty windows casting long, sinister shadows across the floor. Lena swallowed hard, torn between the need to investigate and the urge to escape. She took a cautious step toward the front, the floor creaking beneath her feet, echoing the anxiety that swelled in her chest. As she approached the counter, Lena could see that a display of antique clocks had toppled over, the glass faces shattered and scattered across the floor like shards of time. But there was no one in sight. A chill ran down her spine. She felt an inexplicable dread, as if the very air had thickened with something dark and malevolent. Heart pounding, she glanced back at the journal clutched in her hands. It felt heavy with secrets, as if it were pulsing with life. Determined not to leave empty-handed, she stepped around the debris, careful not to cut herself on the jagged glass. She needed to uncover the truth about the doll—and this journal seemed to be the key. Lena opened the journal again, flipping through the pages until she found a sketch of a ritual. The drawings were intricate, depicting a circle of candles surrounding a doll, each candle marked with a symbol. Lena's breath caught in her throat as she traced the lines with her finger. It was as if the artist had captured some forbidden knowledge, a dark ceremony that promised to awaken the spirits trapped within the porcelain. An icy draft swept through the shop, rustling the pages of the journal. Lena shivered, and for a moment, she thought she saw a figure in the corner of her eye—a fleeting shadow that darted out of sight. She turned quickly, but there was nothing there, just the dimly lit rows of antiques staring back at her like silent witnesses.

"What's happening?" she whispered to herself, desperation clawing at her throat.

She had to understand the connection between the doll and this journal. The unease gnawed at her, and she felt an overwhelming urge to escape the suffocating atmosphere of the shop. Without warning, a loud thud echoed from behind her, making her jump. Lena spun around, flashlight beam slicing through the darkness.

"Is anyone there?" she shouted again, her voice tinged with fear.

There was silence, but the air felt charged, electric. She felt something watching her, an unseen presence lurking just out of sight. Gritting her teeth, she steadied herself and moved toward the back of the shop, hoping to find a clue—anything that could explain the doll's sinister hold over her life. As she reached a dusty shelf lined with oddities, her fingers brushed against a small glass orb. It was filled with swirling black mist, twisting and turning like a dark storm. Lena hesitated, staring at it in wonder and fear. The orb seemed to pulse softly, and for a moment, she felt drawn to it, as if it were whispering secrets to her.

"No," she muttered, shaking her head. "This is insane." But as she turned to leave, the orb rolled slightly on the shelf, a subtle movement that made her blood run cold. The shadows around her deepened, and she felt the chill of a cold breeze whisper past her ear, sending shivers down her spine.

"I need to get out of here," she said, more to herself than anything else. But just as she turned to leave, the lights flickered, plunging the shop into darkness. Panic surged through her as she fumbled for her flashlight, the beam cutting through the heavy gloom.

Then, she saw it—a figure standing at the entrance, silhouetted against the faint light filtering through the front windows. Lena's heart raced. "Who's there?" she called out, trying to keep her voice steady, but it trembled.

The figure stepped forward, revealing the shopkeeper, his face pale and drawn. "You shouldn't be here," he said, his voice urgent and low. "You need to leave. Now."

"Wait!" Lena protested, confusion and fear battling within her. "I found this journal. It's about the doll. I need to understand what's happening!"

The shopkeeper shook his head vehemently, stepping closer. "The doll is cursed. It brings darkness—Malphas seeks a vessel. You must destroy it before it claims you."

His words hit her like a physical blow. Lena felt the weight of his warning settle heavily on her shoulders. "But how? I can't just throw it away! It keeps coming back!"

"You must perform the ritual," he urged, his eyes wide with desperation. "The one in the journal. It is your only chance. But you must hurry. Malphas is powerful, and it will not rest until it has you."

Lena's heart sank. A ritual? What kind of darkness had she unleashed upon herself? But deep down, she felt the urgency of his words, the truth behind them. "Where do I start?" she asked, her voice shaking but determined.

"Gather the materials listed in the journal," he instructed, his voice hushed. "You'll need candles, salt, and a mirror. Go home, and don't let the doll out of your sight. Do not look away."

She nodded, the gravity of the situation settling in. "What about you? Are you safe here?"

His expression darkened. "It's already too late for me. But you—you have a chance. You can end this."

With that, he turned and hurried back toward the entrance, leaving Lena standing there, the journal clutched tightly in her hands. The urgency of her mission weighed heavily on her, but fear nagged at her as well. What had she gotten herself into? As she turned to leave, she couldn't shake the feeling that the shadows were closing in around her, as if the very walls of the shop were alive and suffocating. She stepped out into the cool morning air, gasping as she inhaled the scent of freedom. But there was no relief. The weight of Malphas loomed over her, threatening to snuff out her light. Lena raced to her car, her hands trembling as she unlocked the doors. She glanced back at the shop, half-expecting to see the doll standing in the window, watching her. But there was nothing—just the empty facade of the store, a hollow shell hiding its dark secrets. Once inside the car, she quickly started the engine and pulled away from the curb, the tires squealing on the pavement. The city felt eerily quiet, the streets devoid of the usual morning hustle. As she drove, her thoughts raced. She needed to gather the materials for the ritual, but where would she find them? Candles and salt were easy enough to find, but a mirror? She didn't have one at home. The antique shop had been her best bet, but she couldn't go back there now. Not after everything that had happened. She needed to find a new place—somewhere far away from the darkness that surrounded the doll. Determined, she headed toward the nearest shopping district. As she drove, her mind kept drifting back to the shopkeeper's warning. *Do not look away.* What did he mean? What would happen if she did? She shook her head, trying to push the thoughts aside, but they clung to her like shadows. Arriving at the shopping district, Lena parked the car and quickly made her way into the first store she found—a small convenience shop. She grabbed a pack of candles, a box of salt, and a few snacks to keep her energy up. But the mirror was proving elusive.

"Excuse me," she said to the cashier, an older woman with tired eyes. "Do you sell mirrors?"

The cashier looked up, her brow furrowing. "We have a few in the back. Would you like to take a look?"

"Yes, please," Lena replied, relief flooding her. She followed the woman to a small section in the back, where a couple of dusty mirrors hung on the wall. One in particular caught her eye—a vintage hand mirror with an ornate handle. It felt right, somehow, as if it were calling to her.

"I'll take this one," Lena said, pointing to it. The cashier nodded and rang her up, the sound of the cash register chiming like a warning bell.

"Is everything okay?" the cashier asked, noticing the strain in Lena's voice.

"Yeah, just... a long day," Lena replied, forcing a smile. She didn't want to share her burden with a stranger. "Thank you."

With the items in hand, Lena hurried back to her car, the weight of the journal pressing against her chest. She felt a sense of urgency as she drove back home, the sunlight fading behind dark clouds that gathered ominously in the sky. She had to perform the ritual before nightfall. Arriving home, Lena parked in her driveway and rushed inside, the door slamming shut behind her. She moved to the living room, placing the items on the coffee table. Her heart raced as she opened the journal, flipping to the page with the ritual instructions.

"Gather the candles in a circle," she read aloud, her voice trembling. "Place the salt in the center, and hold the mirror while reciting the incantation." She glanced at the doll, which still sat on the mantel, its cracked face seemingly smirking at her.

With a deep breath, she began to gather the candles, arranging them in a circle on the floor. The flickering light cast dancing shadows on the walls, and she could feel the air around her thickening with tension. Lena placed the salt in the center, creating a barrier that felt almost protective.

Next, she picked up the mirror, its surface gleaming ominously in the candlelight. She could see her reflection staring back, eyes wide with fear and determination. "I can do this," she whispered, steeling herself.

Taking a moment to collect her thoughts, Lena glanced at the journal again, focusing on the incantation. It was an invocation, meant to summon the spirit trapped within the doll. But as she prepared to begin, she felt a rush of doubt. What if this only made things worse?

"Focus," she told herself, shaking her head. "You have to try."

Taking a deep breath, she positioned herself in the center of the circle, holding the mirror in front of her. She could feel the weight of Malphas pressing down on her, an oppressive force that made it difficult to breathe.

"Here goes nothing," she murmured, her voice steadying.

With each word she spoke, Lena felt the air crackle with energy. The candles flickered wildly, and shadows danced around her, as if the room itself was alive and responding to her call.

"Malphas, I summon you," she intoned, feeling the weight of the name echo through her. "Come forth and reveal yourself!"

As the last syllable left her lips, the temperature in the room dropped dramatically. Lena could see her breath condensing in the air, a ghostly vapor that twisted and coiled like smoke. The candles sputtered, their flames flickering in an erratic rhythm. And then, the doll moved. A sudden jolt of fear shot through Lena as she watched the doll's porcelain eyes shift, its cracked mouth curling into a sinister smile.

"You called me," it seemed to whisper, the voice echoing in her mind, a cold breeze swirling around her.

Lena's heart raced, panic flooding her senses. "No, this isn't what I wanted!" she shouted, feeling the shadows closing in tighter, suffocating her. She gripped the mirror, desperately reciting the rest of the incantation, her voice trembling as she fought against the overwhelming presence that threatened to engulf her. The room shook, the walls vibrating as if a great force was being unleashed. Lena felt the power of the ritual surge around her, and she closed her eyes, focusing on the mirror. She had to stand firm, to confront whatever darkness lay beyond.

"Leave me!" she cried, summoning every ounce of strength within her. "You have no power here!"

But as she shouted, the shadows surged forward, coiling around her like tendrils, pulling her toward the depths of despair. Lena gasped, fighting against the invisible grip, but it was too late. The doll's laughter echoed in her mind, a chilling sound that promised nothing but torment. With a final surge of determination, she raised the mirror high, reflecting the candlelight in a blinding flash.

"I command you to return to the darkness!" she shouted, her voice ringing through the chaos.

In that moment, the world erupted around her, the shadows recoiling as a blinding light filled the room. Lena felt the power of the ritual surge, pushing against the darkness that threatened to consume her. She would not be a vessel for Malphas. Not now, not ever. And then, with a deafening roar, the darkness shattered, leaving her gasping on the floor, the candles flickering softly in the aftermath. She lay there, panting, the mirror clattering to the ground as the shadows dissolved into the corners of the room. Silence enveloped her, and she slowly opened her eyes, the weight of the darkness lifting. But as she looked around, the doll remained on the mantel, its expression unchanged—a cracked smile, a hollow gaze. Lena's heart sank as she realized the truth: this was only the beginning.

Chapter 6

Lena lay on the floor, her chest heaving as the remnants of the ritual hung in the air like a heavy fog. The silence pressed in on her, oppressive and disorienting. She felt as if she had been thrust into a nightmare from which she could not wake. The doll remained on the mantel, its porcelain face unchanged, but there was an unmistakable shift in the atmosphere. It felt charged, electric, as if the very walls of her home had absorbed the remnants of Malphas's power. She pushed herself up, trembling as she tried to gather her thoughts. What had just happened? Had she succeeded in driving the darkness away, or merely scratched the surface of an ancient evil? Lena's mind raced with questions, each one more frightening than the last. The mirror lay shattered on the floor, its surface reflecting shards of flickering candlelight. She swallowed hard, feeling a knot of guilt twist in her stomach. Had she released something she couldn't control? A cold sweat broke out across her forehead as she recalled the moment the doll had laughed, a chilling sound that echoed in her mind.

"Get a grip," she muttered to herself, pushing off the floor and grabbing a towel to clean up the broken mirror. "You need to focus." But even as she spoke, her hands shook, and her breath quickened. The lingering presence of Malphas hung like a shroud, making her skin crawl.

As she cleaned the shards, her thoughts turned to the shopkeeper's warning. "It's already too late for me." What had he meant? Had the doll claimed his soul? With every moment that passed, Lena felt the weight of the darkness pressing in on her, a relentless reminder that she was far from safe.

Once the mess was cleaned up, she sat on the couch, clutching the journal tightly in her lap. The pages felt warm against her fingers, a stark contrast to the chill in the air. She flipped through the entries again, searching for answers—anything that could shed light on what she had just encountered.

One entry stood out, written in a frantic scrawl. It detailed the artist's descent into madness, the voices that whispered in the night, urging him to bring the doll to life. "Malphas is a demon of the forgotten, a trickster who feeds on fear," he wrote. "He thrives in the shadows, seeking vessels to do his bidding."

Lena's heart raced as she read the words. She was not merely a victim but a potential vessel for something far more sinister. Her gaze drifted to the doll, which sat innocently on the mantel, its expression frozen in a haunting smile. She felt a chill run down her spine. The ritual had been a mistake. Determined to confront this darkness head-on, Lena opened the journal to the last page, where the final incantation was written. "To banish Malphas, one must confront their greatest fear."

"What's my greatest fear?" Lena whispered to herself.

The answer hung heavy in the air, waiting to be acknowledged. She had been running from her past, from the trauma of her childhood and the shadows that loomed over her life. But could she face that fear now? Closing her eyes, Lena took a deep breath, allowing memories to flood her mind. Images of her childhood home surfaced, the dark corners of her room where she had felt unseen eyes watching her. The loneliness, the fear of abandonment. The night her mother had left. That moment had marked her, carving deep scars that still throbbed beneath the surface. Suddenly, the sound of laughter pulled her from her reverie. Lena's eyes flew open, her heart racing. It was a soft, haunting laugh—faint but unmistakable—echoing from the living room. She glanced toward the mantel where the doll rested, and her breath caught in her throat. The doll was no longer still. It appeared to be swaying slightly, its eyes glimmering with a life of their own. Lena felt her pulse quicken as she stood up, instinctively backing away. "No... this can't be happening."

"Lena..." the doll whispered, its voice like the rustling of dead leaves. "You invited me here."

"No!" she shouted, shaking her head furiously. "I didn't mean it! I want you gone!"

The doll's cracked face split into a wider grin, revealing jagged teeth that shouldn't have been there. "But you're afraid, and fear is my domain. You can't escape me, Lena. I am part of you now."

Lena felt a surge of rage mixed with fear. "You're just a doll! You can't hurt me!" But the trembling in her voice betrayed her bravado. The shadows in the room began to thicken, swirling around her like a dark mist, and she realized that she was not just facing the doll; she was confronting her own demons.

"No, Lena," the doll crooned, its voice dripping with mockery. "You've always known the truth. You were never alone in your fear. I've been waiting for this moment."

In that instant, Lena remembered the darkness that had loomed over her life since childhood. The shadows that had clung to her, the whispers of self-doubt that echoed in her mind, telling her she wasn't good enough. She had spent years fighting against that darkness, trying to bury it deep within, but it was never truly gone.

"Leave me alone!" Lena screamed, her voice breaking. She could feel the tears welling up in her eyes, the weight of her fear crashing down upon her like a tidal wave. "I won't let you take me!"

But the doll merely chuckled, a chilling sound that echoed through the room. "You can't fight what you are, Lena. I will show you your true self. Embrace me."

Suddenly, the room spun, and Lena felt herself being pulled into the darkness. She gasped, struggling against the invisible force that gripped her tightly. The walls around her melted away, and she was thrust into a world of shadows, where the air was thick and oppressive. Lena found herself standing in a dark, twisted version of her childhood home. The familiar layout was warped and grotesque, shadows lurking in every corner. The air was heavy with despair, a palpable weight that threatened to suffocate her.

"Welcome home," the doll's voice echoed, reverberating through the suffocating darkness. "This is where it all began, Lena."

"Get out!" she shouted, but her voice echoed back, swallowed by the shadows. She felt the overwhelming presence of her past crashing over her, memories flooding back unbidden—her mother's anger, the screams, the loneliness that followed.

"Face them," the doll urged, its voice a whisper that slithered into her mind. "Embrace your fears. Only then will you be free."

As the shadows closed in, Lena felt her heart race. This was her chance to confront everything she had buried for so long. "I won't let you control me," she declared, summoning the remnants of her strength. "I am more than my fears!"

With that thought in mind, Lena pushed back against the darkness, refusing to succumb to its oppressive weight. She focused on the memories that haunted her, the moments of pain and sorrow, and one by one, she began to confront them.

The first shadow flickered before her—a young girl, no older than eight, sitting alone in a corner, tears streaming down her face. It was her, the girl she had long forgotten. "You're not alone," Lena whispered, kneeling beside her younger self. "You're stronger than this. We can get through it together."

The shadow shifted, flickering like a flame, and for a moment, Lena felt a warmth envelop her. The little girl looked up, her eyes wide with surprise. "Who are you?" she asked, her voice trembling.

"I'm you," Lena replied, her heart swelling with compassion. "I'm here to remind you that you are not alone. We can fight this together."

With each memory she faced, the shadows began to recede. The darkness that had once loomed over her life began to dissolve, replaced by a flickering light that grew stronger with every confrontation. Lena felt a surge of empowerment, the weight of her fears lifting as she acknowledged her pain.

But then the laughter returned, cold and mocking. "You think you can escape me? I am your fear, your darkness. You cannot banish me!"

"I can!" Lena shouted, her voice ringing out against the oppressive shadows. "I choose to confront you! You do not own me!"

With every ounce of strength, she pushed forward, a light blossoming in her chest. The shadows writhed, and the doll's laughter turned to shrieks of rage as the darkness began to shatter around her. The twisted house melted away, replaced by the memories of laughter and joy she had hidden away for too long.

"I am not defined by you," she declared, her voice steady and resolute. "I choose to embrace my light!"

With that final proclamation, the darkness erupted, dissolving into a million tiny specks of shadow that danced in the air before fading into nothingness. Lena stood in the empty space, her heart racing, but a sense of peace enveloped her. She was free—free from the chains of her past, free from the hold of Malphas. But as the dust settled, the laughter faded, and she opened her eyes, the doll remained on the mantel, its smile wider than before.

"You think this is over?" it taunted, the voice dripping with malice. "This is only the beginning, Lena. You may have faced the past, but you will never escape me."

Lena's heart sank, a chill running down her spine. The battle was far from over, and deep within her, she felt the shadows stirring again. She knew she had won a significant victory, but Malphas was not easily defeated.

Determined, she clenched her fists, her resolve hardening. "I will find a way to banish you," she vowed, staring defiantly at the doll. "You will not control me!"

And as she turned away, a flicker of doubt gnawed at her. She had faced her fears, but the darkness was a cunning adversary. Could she truly banish Malphas, or would it continue to haunt her, lurking in the shadows, waiting for the moment she would falter? Only time would tell, and Lena was prepared to fight.

Chapter 7

Lena awoke the next morning, sunlight filtering through her curtains, illuminating the dust motes that danced in the air. It felt like a new beginning, a fresh start after the chaos of the previous night. Yet, despite the warmth of the sun, a chilling unease settled in her gut. The remnants of her encounter with Malphas still lingered in her mind, and she couldn't shake the feeling that the battle was far from over. Sitting up, she rubbed her temples, trying to dispel the remnants of a restless night. Shadows had flickered in her dreams, twisted shapes that whispered her name and promised darkness. She had faced her fears, but the victory felt hollow. The doll still sat on the mantel, a silent witness to her struggle, and she could sense its presence pressing down on her, a reminder that Malphas was still lurking, biding its time. Determined to take control of her life, Lena pushed the covers off and stood. She needed answers, and she needed to strengthen her resolve. After her confrontation, she had vowed to find a way to banish Malphas for good. She couldn't afford to let her guard down. After a quick shower and a breakfast of toast and coffee, Lena sat at her kitchen table, the journal open before her. She flipped through the pages, searching for anything she might have missed, any detail that could give her insight into the doll's true nature. Each entry seemed to taunt her, a reminder of the darkness she was facing. Then, one entry caught her attention—a passage detailing the history of the doll and the artist who had created it. It spoke of a tragic tale of love and loss, a man consumed by grief after the death of his beloved. In his desperation, he had turned to dark magic, creating Malphas as a means to resurrect her spirit. The artist had believed that by binding her essence to the doll, he could cheat death itself. But the ritual had gone horribly wrong. Instead of bringing his love back, he had awakened something far more sinister, a demon that thrived on despair and fear.

"This isn't just a doll," Lena murmured, her fingers tracing the words. "It's a vessel for something much darker."

A chill ran through her as she considered the implications. Malphas was not only a trickster but a manipulator of emotions—an entity that fed on fear, grief, and loneliness. She had experienced its influence firsthand, the whispers that taunted her in the dark, urging her to succumb to despair. The memory of the doll's laughter echoed in her mind, sending shivers down her spine. Lena closed her eyes, taking a deep breath to center herself. She needed to find a way to sever the bond between Malphas and the doll. The key lay in understanding its origins and the artist's tragic tale. With newfound determination, Lena grabbed her phone and began to research the artist, his life, and the events surrounding the doll's creation. Hours passed as she scoured the internet, piecing together fragments of information. The artist had vanished without a trace, leaving behind only the doll and the haunting stories of those who had encountered it. One article mentioned a local legend that spoke of a hidden shrine, where the artist had performed the final ritual to bind his love to the doll. The shrine was said to be a place of great power, imbued with the remnants of the dark magic he had wielded. Lena's heart raced at the thought of visiting the shrine. It could be the key to breaking the bond between Malphas and the doll. But would she be able to confront the darkness that lingered there? The risk was immense, but she knew she had to try. After a quick glance at the clock, Lena grabbed her jacket and headed out the door. The sun hung high in the sky, casting long shadows on the pavement as she walked. Each step felt like a leap into the unknown, but the thrill of discovery pushed her forward. The path led her to the outskirts of town, where the landscape changed from bustling streets to overgrown paths and the dense woods that surrounded the abandoned shrine. As she approached the area described in the article, the atmosphere shifted. The trees grew denser, their branches twisting overhead like skeletal fingers reaching for the sky. A sense of foreboding settled in, a whisper of warning that echoed in her mind. Lena paused for a moment, glancing back at the town behind her, the safety of familiarity feeling like a distant memory.

"No turning back," she whispered to herself, taking a deep breath before stepping deeper into the woods.

The sound of her footsteps crunched against the leaves, and with every step, she felt the weight of anticipation building. The shrine came into view, a crumbling stone structure overgrown with vines and moss. It looked like a remnant of a forgotten time, its once-proud facade now a shadow of its former glory. Lena felt a chill run down her spine as she approached, the air thick with an unsettling energy. Pushing open the creaking door, Lena stepped inside. The interior was dimly lit, shadows clinging to the corners like dark secrets waiting to be unearthed. The walls were adorned with faded symbols and runes, remnants of the dark magic that had once pulsed through this place. In the center stood an altar, worn and cracked, a darkened stain marking its surface—a testament to the rituals performed long ago. Lena felt her heart race as she approached the altar. She could sense the lingering energy, a pulse that thrummed beneath her feet. It was both alluring and terrifying, a reminder of the power that once filled this space. With trembling hands, she reached out, tracing the symbols carved into the stone.

"Show me the truth," she whispered, feeling the weight of her words in the heavy silence. "Let me understand what was lost."

As she spoke, a gust of wind swept through the shrine, extinguishing the light that filtered through the cracked windows. The shadows deepened, and Lena's breath caught in her throat. The atmosphere shifted, thickening with an oppressive weight that felt almost sentient, wrapping around her like a suffocating shroud.

"Lena..." a voice whispered, a sound that echoed through the chamber, sending chills racing down her spine. "You seek the truth, but are you prepared for what you will find?"

"Who's there?" Lena demanded, her voice echoing off the walls. She felt the shadows closing in, pressing against her skin, and she refused to let fear take hold. "Show yourself!"

In response, the air shimmered, and the figure of a woman emerged from the shadows, ethereal and hauntingly beautiful. Her long hair floated around her, a cascade of dark tendrils that seemed to dance with the shadows. Lena's heart raced as she realized the woman resembled the doll, a ghostly likeness that sent a jolt of recognition through her.

"I am the spirit bound to the doll," the woman spoke, her voice both soothing and mournful. "I was trapped by the artist's desperate love, a victim of his folly."

"Why are you here?" Lena asked, her voice trembling. "What do you want?"

The woman's gaze pierced through Lena, a mixture of sorrow and longing in her eyes. "I cannot leave until the bond is broken, until the darkness that has tainted this place is purged. Malphas feeds on our pain, our despair. He twists our memories to keep us bound to this realm."

Lena's heart sank as she understood. The doll was not merely a vessel for Malphas; it was also a prison for the spirit of the woman before her. "How can I help you?" Lena asked, desperation creeping into her voice. "What do I need to do?"

The spirit's expression softened, a flicker of hope igniting in her eyes. "To free me, you must confront the darkness that binds us. The final ritual must be performed at the moment of the eclipse, when the veil between worlds is thinnest. Only then can Malphas be vanquished."

"But how do I perform the ritual?" Lena pressed, her mind racing with the enormity of the task ahead. "I can't do this alone."

"You are not alone," the spirit replied, her voice a gentle caress. "The strength within you is greater than you realize. Remember the light you found within your fears. Use it to confront Malphas, to challenge him at his core."

As the spirit's words sank in, Lena felt a surge of determination rise within her. She could do this. She would find a way to banish Malphas and free the spirit trapped within the doll.

"I will do it," Lena declared, her voice steady. "I'll confront Malphas and perform the ritual."

The spirit smiled, a fleeting glimpse of joy amidst her sorrow. "You must gather the necessary components—a mirror, a candle, and a lock of hair from the doll. Together, they will form the catalyst needed to bind Malphas once and for all."

Lena's heart raced as she committed the components to memory. She would return home, prepare for the ritual, and face the darkness head-on. This was her chance to reclaim her life and free the spirit that had suffered for too long.

But just as hope blossomed within her, the air shifted again, heavy with foreboding. "Be cautious, Lena," the spirit warned, her expression turning grave. "Malphas will not let you leave easily. He will come for you. You must be prepared."

A cold gust of wind swept through the shrine, extinguishing the light that had flickered within. The spirit began to fade, her form dissolving into the shadows. "Trust in your strength," she urged, her voice echoing in the darkness. "And remember, you are not alone."

As the last remnants of the spirit vanished, Lena felt a sense of urgency wash over her. She needed to leave, to prepare for the battle ahead. Turning on her heel, she dashed toward the exit, the shadows closing in around her like a tightening noose. Outside, the air was crisp and cool, a stark contrast to the oppressive darkness she had just left behind. Lena took a deep breath, grounding herself in the reality of the moment. She could feel the weight of the doll's presence lingering at the back of her mind, a reminder of the impending confrontation. Determined to gather the components needed for the ritual, Lena raced home, her heart pounding in her chest. She knew that the time for the final showdown was drawing near, and she would face Malphas with every ounce of strength she possessed.

Chapter 8

As Lena approached her home, the weight of her decision settled heavily on her shoulders. The revelation of the spirit's plight burned brightly in her mind, fueling her determination but also intensifying her fear. She could still feel the chill in the air, the lingering shadows from the shrine haunting her every step. The doll, now more than ever, felt like a looming specter in her life, its presence as constant as the heartbeat in her chest. The front door creaked open, and Lena stepped inside, her heart racing as she locked the door behind her. The warmth of the sun seemed to dissipate the moment she crossed the threshold, replaced by a foreboding silence that enveloped her. It was as if the walls themselves were watching, waiting for the inevitable clash between light and darkness. She glanced at the mantel where the doll sat, its painted smile somehow more sinister than before. Taking a deep breath, Lena forced herself to look away. "I won't let you win," she whispered, the words a promise as much to herself as to the malevolent force that lurked in the corners of her mind. With resolve hardening in her chest, Lena moved toward her bedroom, where she had laid out the components for the ritual. The mirror, the candle, and the lock of hair were waiting for her, a trio of artifacts that would either save her or plunge her deeper into despair. She knew she needed to gather more supplies and prepare her mind for the confrontation ahead. First, Lena took the mirror—a small, hand-held piece with a silver frame, its glass still reflecting the remnants of her resolve. It was said that a mirror could reveal hidden truths, reflecting not just the physical but the emotional and spiritual states of those who gazed into it. She felt it was fitting, as she would be looking into it during the ritual to confront Malphas. Next, she turned her attention to the candle—a black, tapered candle that seemed to absorb the light around it. The darkness it emitted felt almost alive, a potent reminder of the malevolent force she was about to challenge. She would need its power to focus her intent and channel her energy. Lastly, the lock of hair from the doll, carefully cut and preserved, sat in a small glass vial on her nightstand. It served as a direct link to Malphas, a tether that would allow her to confront the darkness that bound them both.

As she gathered the items, Lena's thoughts wandered back to the spirit she had encountered at the shrine. What had she meant by trusting in her strength? What did it truly mean to confront Malphas? The memory of the spirit's haunting beauty lingered in her mind. It had been a powerful reminder of the sorrow that had birthed the darkness—a woman consumed by love and desperation, now trapped within the very thing that had once brought her joy. Lena felt a pang of sympathy, a connection forged by their shared suffering. She wasn't just fighting for herself; she was fighting for the spirit's freedom as well. Determined to fortify her mind, Lena sat cross-legged on the floor, surrounding herself with the components of the ritual. She closed her eyes and took a deep breath, allowing the weight of her thoughts to settle. With each inhale, she focused on the light within her, the flicker of hope that had ignited when she first encountered the spirit. In her mind, she pictured the light expanding, filling the space around her, pushing back against the shadows that threatened to close in. She envisioned it illuminating the path ahead, guiding her through the darkness.

"Let the light guide me," she whispered, her voice steady. "Let it show me the truth."

Images began to swirl behind her eyelids—flickering lights, shadowy figures, and the doll's unnerving smile. Lena felt a surge of energy coursing through her, a powerful reminder that she was not alone in this fight. The strength she had found within herself during her darkest moments surged forth, merging with the light she had summoned. But as she focused on the light, she felt something else lurking just beyond her reach—an insidious presence that sought to snuff out her flame. Malphas was not idle. It was watching, waiting for the perfect moment to strike. A sudden chill raced through the room, and Lena's eyes flew open. The shadows seemed to pulse around her, thick and oppressive, as if Malphas were trying to break through the barrier she had created. Panic flared within her, but she quickly steeled herself. She wouldn't let fear take control. Not now.

"I will not be afraid," she declared, her voice ringing out with newfound confidence. "I am stronger than you, Malphas!"

The shadows writhed in response, a low growl echoing through the room, the air thick with malice. Lena's heart raced, but she held her ground, the light within her flaring brighter in defiance. The whispers of doubt clawed at her mind, urging her to give in, but she refused to listen.

"Show yourself!" she shouted, clenching her fists. "Face me if you dare!"

The shadows coalesced, swirling around her like a storm, and for a moment, Lena felt a flicker of fear. But then, she remembered the spirit's words—the strength within her was greater than she realized. Drawing upon that well of power, she pushed back against the encroaching darkness. And then, suddenly, the room fell silent. Lena stood in the stillness, the air thick with tension. For a moment, it felt as if the world had paused, the shadows holding their breath. She could almost feel the presence of Malphas hovering just beyond the edge of her perception, waiting, watching. Determined to keep the momentum going, Lena set to work gathering the rest of her supplies. She wrote down the necessary incantations she had found during her research, words that would focus her intent during the ritual. As she scrawled them across the pages of her journal, she could almost hear the echoes of the spirits surrounding her, their collective energy urging her forward. After hours of preparation, Lena felt exhaustion creep in, her body weary from the emotional toll of the day. She had gathered everything she needed, but her mind buzzed with anxiety, the clock ticking down toward the eclipse. She needed rest, but sleep felt like an impossible luxury. Sitting on the edge of her bed, Lena stared at the clock as the minutes slipped away. The darkness would soon envelop the world outside, and with it, her final chance to confront Malphas. Finally, as the sun began to dip below the horizon, casting long shadows through her window, Lena took a deep breath and made her way to the mantel. She picked up the doll, feeling its cold porcelain skin against her fingertips. Its smile seemed to mock her, but she refused to flinch.

"Tonight," she whispered fiercely, "you will be banished."

The candle flickered ominously as she placed the doll next to it, the room now drenched in a dusky glow. The ritual was about to begin, and she could feel the air thickening with anticipation. Outside, the first stars twinkled in the deepening twilight, a reminder of the battle that lay ahead. She would not face this darkness alone. As she arranged the components of the ritual, Lena closed her eyes and reached deep within herself, calling upon the strength she had found in her darkest moments. The echoes of the spirit's words rang in her mind, a mantra of hope and defiance.

"I will confront you, Malphas," she vowed, her voice steady. "I will reclaim my life and free the spirit trapped within you."

The shadows around her shifted, and for a moment, the world felt charged with energy. She opened her eyes, resolute, ready to embrace the chaos and confront the darkness that had haunted her for too long. With the eclipse drawing near, Lena knew that the time for hesitation had passed. She would face Malphas and fight for both her freedom and the freedom of the spirit she had come to understand.

Chapter 9

The atmosphere in Lena's room was thick with anticipation as she arranged the final components for the ritual. The flickering candle cast dancing shadows across the walls, creating an eerie backdrop for the confrontation that was about to unfold. Outside, the sky had deepened into a rich navy, the first hints of the eclipse starting to cloak the moon in darkness. Lena could feel the pull of the celestial event, a magnetic force urging her to step forward, to embrace the chaos of the moment. She had read about the power of eclipses in her research—a time when the veil between the physical and spiritual realms was thinnest. Tonight, she would harness that power. With a deep breath, she focused on the mirror, positioning it in front of her so that it caught the light from the candle. She had read that during the ritual, the mirror could reflect more than just her physical appearance; it would reveal her inner strength and the true nature of Malphas. With it, she could confront the demon and, hopefully, find a way to sever the bond that tethered them together. As the minutes ticked away, Lena felt the tension in the air growing thicker, almost palpable. Shadows seemed to writhe and shift, almost alive in their pursuit of her fear. She could hear faint whispers, echoes of voices long gone, rising and falling in a sinister rhythm. Her heart raced, and she reminded herself to breathe. This was not the time to succumb to panic. She had a purpose, a goal, and she would see it through. Lena picked up the vial containing the lock of hair from the doll. Its glass felt cool against her palm, a reminder of the connection she shared with Malphas. "This ends tonight," she whispered, determination hardening her resolve. She placed the vial on the floor before her, ensuring it was within reach during the ritual. Next, she reached for the incantation she had meticulously copied into her journal. The words were powerful, infused with the energy of the spirits who had guided her thus far. Each syllable resonated with meaning, and she could almost feel the weight of the spirits behind her, urging her onward. Finally, she lit the black candle, watching as the flame flickered and grew, its darkness seeming to consume the light around it. "Let the shadows guide me," she murmured, placing her hands on her knees as she settled into a meditative position. As the candle burned, the shadows danced in erratic patterns, swirling like a tempest in the room. Lena closed her eyes, concentrating on the incantation. She could feel the air humming around her, charged with energy as the eclipse neared its peak. The world outside seemed to dim in response, the moon eclipsing the sun, casting an otherworldly pall over everything.

"By the light of the moon and the darkness of night, I summon the strength within to face the blight," she began, her voice steady and clear. The words flowed from her lips, imbued with purpose. With each line, she felt a connection to the energy around her, the pull of the eclipse drawing her deeper into the ritual.

As she continued the incantation, Lena felt the temperature drop, an unnatural chill seeping into the room. The shadows thickened, coiling around her like serpents, their whispers rising to a fever pitch. "Come forth, Malphas," she intoned, the invocation echoing through the air. Suddenly, the shadows surged, coalescing into a dark figure before her. Lena's heart pounded in her chest, but she held her ground, the light of the candle flickering defiantly against the encroaching darkness. The figure took shape, revealing a menacing silhouette with piercing eyes that glowed like embers in the night.

"Foolish girl," Malphas hissed, its voice a haunting melody that sent shivers down her spine. "You dare summon me?"

Lena met the creature's gaze, steeling her nerves. "I do dare," she declared, her voice unwavering. "You will no longer hold sway over my life or the spirit you've tormented. I am here to end this."

A low, mocking laugh echoed through the room, reverberating against the walls. "You believe you can free the spirit? She is bound to me, as are you. Your strength is nothing compared to my power."

"I have the strength of the spirits behind me," Lena countered, the words pouring forth with renewed conviction. "I will sever the bond that ties us. You will not take another soul."

Malphas's eyes narrowed, a glimmer of anger flickering within their depths. "You think yourself worthy of such a task? You are merely a child playing with forces beyond your comprehension."

As the demon spoke, Lena felt the shadows tighten around her, pressing in like a vise. Panic clawed at her throat, but she pushed it back, focusing on the light she had summoned within herself. "I am more than a child," she shouted, her voice echoing in defiance. "I am the one who will end your reign of terror!"

With a swift movement, Lena reached for the mirror, holding it up to Malphas. The reflection shimmered, revealing not just the demon's dark visage but the swirling energy of the eclipse behind it. The power surged through her, a tangible force that crackled in the air, intertwining with her intent.

"By the light of the moon and the dark of the night," she continued, "I cast you out into the void. You will no longer haunt this world or the spirit you've consumed!"

As she spoke the final words of her incantation, Lena felt the candle flicker wildly, the flame threatening to extinguish. But she held firm, channeling every ounce of her strength into the mirror. The glass caught the light, reflecting it back at Malphas, illuminating the darkness that enveloped him.

The demon roared, a sound that shook the very foundations of her home. "You cannot do this! You are mine!"

But Lena could feel the energy coalescing, a powerful wave of light that surged from within her and through the mirror. "I am not yours!" she shouted, unleashing the energy in a brilliant burst. The shadows recoiled, the light washing over them like a cleansing tide.

At that moment, Lena felt an overwhelming surge of power course through her veins, fueled by the connection she had forged with the spirits. She was not alone; she was a conduit for their strength, and together, they would banish Malphas from her life. The shadows writhed and twisted, fighting against the light. Malphas's form began to flicker, its dark essence unraveling under the intensity of Lena's resolve. "No! This cannot be!" it screamed, its voice echoing in a cacophony of fury and despair.

But Lena refused to back down. "I release you!" she shouted, her voice ringing clear above the chaos. "I sever the bond!"

With one final surge of energy, she directed the light from the mirror straight at Malphas, the brilliance overwhelming the darkness. The room exploded in a blinding flash as the shadows dissipated, swallowed by the light. When the brightness faded, Lena collapsed to the floor, breathless and trembling. The air felt different now, lighter somehow, as if a great weight had been lifted. She glanced around her room, half-expecting to see Malphas still lurking in the shadows. But it was gone. The oppressive darkness had lifted, replaced by a serene calm that enveloped her. Lena closed her eyes, relief flooding through her. She had done it—she had confronted the darkness and emerged victorious. As she lay on the floor, her heart racing, she felt a gentle presence wash over her. It was familiar and warm, a comforting sensation that soothed her weary spirit. The bond she had forged with the spirit at the shrine lingered, filling her with a sense of peace.

"I am free," a soft voice echoed in her mind, the words reverberating with gratitude. "Thank you, Lena."

Tears prickled at Lena's eyes as she realized the spirit was finally free. She had not only fought for her own life but for the life of another.

The shadows had retreated, leaving behind the promise of a new beginning. With newfound strength, Lena pushed herself up from the floor, the remnants of the ritual still buzzing in the air around her. She looked at the mirror, its surface reflecting her tired but determined face.

"I did it," she whispered, disbelief mingling with triumph. "I really did it."

But the journey was far from over. The eclipse had passed, but Lena knew there were still remnants of the darkness that lingered, and the healing process had only just begun. She would need to confront her own fears, to rebuild the life that had been shattered.

As she gathered her strength, Lena made a silent vow to honor the spirit she had freed. She would learn from this experience, using the light she had discovered within herself to guide her moving forward. Tonight had changed her. She would not forget the shadows, nor the darkness she had faced, but she would not be defined by them. With a determined heart, Lena stood up and began to clean the remnants of the ritual. The darkness had been vanquished, and though scars would remain, she was ready to embrace the journey ahead—one filled with light, hope, and the promise of healing.

Chapter 10

The stillness of Lena's room felt surreal in the wake of the tumultuous confrontation with Malphas. The remnants of the ritual lay scattered across the floor—candle wax dripped like tears, the mirror reflected her own weary image, and the vial of hair glimmered innocently in the soft light. She had won, yet a hollow ache lingered within her, a bittersweet reminder of what she had faced and the price of her victory. Lena sat on the edge of her bed, staring into the mirror as she struggled to reconcile her emotions. The shadows had been vanquished, but the fear they had instilled in her still coiled tightly in her chest. She had confronted Malphas and severed the bond that had trapped her, yet the specter of her own darkness loomed larger than ever. What did it mean to be free? Would she ever feel truly safe again? The echoes of the ritual reverberated in her mind, every incantation and every word exchanged with Malphas replaying in an endless loop. "I am not yours," she had declared, but the truth was far more complex. She had fought against a demon, but in doing so, she had also fought against her own fears, insecurities, and the shadows of her past. Lena took a deep breath, grounding herself in the moment. She needed to process what had happened. Instead of allowing the fear to wash over her like a tide, she resolved to confront it head-on. Picking up her journal from the bedside table, she flipped to a fresh page, the crisp paper waiting for her thoughts. As she began to write, the words flowed like a cathartic river, carrying with them the weight of her experience.

Tonight, I confronted Malphas. I faced the darkness that had haunted me for so long. I fought for myself, but I also fought for the spirit trapped within the doll. I did not succumb to fear. I found my strength.

With each line, she felt the tension in her body begin to ease. Writing had always been a refuge, a safe space where she could explore her emotions without judgment. It was a way to process the chaos swirling in her mind, transforming pain into something tangible, something she could understand.

But the fight is not over. I have emerged victorious, yet the shadows still linger. I must learn to confront them. I must learn to embrace my own light.

As the ink dried on the page, Lena felt a shift within her. The act of writing had empowered her, allowing her to take ownership of her experience and assert her will against the remnants of fear that clung to her like a shadow. She had faced Malphas, and though he had been vanquished, the echoes of his influence were not so easily erased. Suddenly, a soft chime broke the silence, and Lena's heart skipped a beat. The sound of her phone vibrating on the nightstand pulled her from her thoughts. She reached for it, surprised to see a message from Claire, her closest friend.

Hey! Just checking in. How are you holding up?

A wave of warmth washed over Lena at the thought of Claire's unwavering support. Though she had kept her experiences hidden from her friends, the bond they shared had always been a source of comfort. She hesitated for a moment, contemplating how much to share.

I'm okay, just had a rough night. Can we talk?

Claire's response was almost immediate. *Of course! I'm on my way over. Be there in 10!*

The prospect of having someone to talk to filled Lena with a mix of relief and apprehension. She had spent so long battling her demons alone, and the thought of opening up felt both liberating and terrifying. What would she even say? How could she explain the horrors she had faced, the darkness that had invaded her life? She stood up, pacing her room as she waited for Claire to arrive. The walls felt like they were closing in on her, a reminder of the isolation she had endured. It was time to share her burden, to let someone in. The minutes stretched like hours, and as Lena glanced out the window, she noted the way the moon hung low in the sky, a ghostly presence in the aftermath of the eclipse. It felt as if the universe were reflecting her inner turmoil—beautiful yet haunting, filled with potential but shadowed by uncertainty. Finally, there was a soft knock at the door, and Lena's heart raced. She opened it to find Claire standing there, her face lit up with concern and affection.

"Hey! I came as soon as I could," she said, stepping inside. "You look... well, not great. What happened?"

Lena offered a weak smile, grateful for her friend's presence. "It's a long story," she admitted, her voice wavering slightly. "But I think I really need to talk about it."

Claire nodded, her expression shifting from concern to understanding. "I'm all ears. Just tell me what you're comfortable sharing."

They settled onto the bed, Lena's heart pounding in her chest as she began to recount the events of the night. The words tumbled from her lips, raw and unfiltered. She described the ritual, the confrontation with Malphas, and the release of the spirit. Claire listened intently, her eyes wide with shock and empathy.

"Wow, Lena," Claire finally said, her voice filled with awe. "You're so brave. I can't believe you faced something like that alone."

"I didn't feel brave at the time," Lena admitted, her voice trembling. "It was terrifying. I felt so small in the face of it all."

"But you did it," Claire insisted, placing a comforting hand on Lena's shoulder. "You fought back. You didn't let the darkness win."

"I guess," Lena replied, her eyes drifting toward the doll perched on the mantel. "But I still feel... changed. The fear is still there, lingering. I don't know how to move past it."

Claire studied her for a moment, a thoughtful expression crossing her face. "Healing takes time. You've been through something traumatic, and it's okay to feel scared or uncertain. Just don't try to carry it all alone. You have people who care about you."

Lena felt the warmth of Claire's words wash over her, and for the first time since the confrontation, she felt a flicker of hope. "Thank you," she whispered, her heart swelling with gratitude. "I don't know what I would do without you."

They sat in comfortable silence for a few moments, Lena feeling the weight of her burdens lighten just a bit. It was liberating to share her experience, to not have to bear the burden alone. But as the quiet stretched on, Lena's mind began to race again. What would happen next? Would Malphas return? Would the darkness rise again? She needed to be prepared for whatever came next.

"Claire," Lena began hesitantly, breaking the silence. "Do you believe in the supernatural? In spirits and demons?"

Claire raised an eyebrow, clearly intrigued. "I mean, I'm open to the idea. Why?"

Lena took a deep breath, gathering her thoughts. "Because I think I may have to confront the remnants of Malphas. The shadows haven't fully left, and I can't shake the feeling that this isn't over yet."

Claire's expression shifted from curiosity to concern. "What do you mean? Do you think he's still out there?"

"I don't know," Lena admitted. "But I feel it in my bones. There's still a connection, and I need to be ready for whatever comes next. I can't let my guard down."

Claire nodded, her brows furrowing in thought. "So, what's your plan?"

"I want to research more about Malphas, about spirits and demons," Lena replied, determination flooding her voice. "I need to understand what I'm dealing with and how to protect myself."

"Sounds like a plan," Claire said, her tone encouraging. "We can hit the library together, or I can help you search online. You don't have to do this alone."

The offer warmed Lena's heart, and she felt a renewed sense of purpose. "I'd like that. I think I need a partner in this."

As they began to discuss their next steps, Lena felt a sense of camaraderie blossom between them. The darkness she had faced was still present, lurking at the edges of her consciousness, but she no longer felt isolated in her struggle. With Claire by her side, she felt stronger, more capable of confronting the unknown. The night deepened around them, the shadows settling back into their corners, but Lena could feel the light within her pushing back against the darkness. The echoes of Malphas might linger, but she would no longer allow them to define her. Together, they would uncover the truth, armed with knowledge and the strength of their friendship. The journey ahead would be fraught with challenges, but Lena was ready to face whatever lay ahead. She would not let fear control her life; instead, she would wield it as a weapon, turning her pain into power. As they plotted their course, the room felt alive with possibility, a vibrant space where hope and determination could thrive. With her heart full of resolve, Lena knew she would emerge from this darkness, stronger than ever.

Chapter 11

The following morning, the sun broke through the remnants of the night, casting a warm golden light across Lena's room. As she stirred from a restless sleep, the memories of her encounter with Malphas flooded back, intertwining with the remnants of her dreams. Lena sat up, feeling the weight of the world pressing down on her shoulders, but today, she was determined to face it head-on. After a quick breakfast, Lena met Claire at the local library. The familiar smell of aged paper and ink wrapped around them like a comforting embrace. They headed to the research section, where the towering shelves seemed to hold endless secrets, just waiting to be uncovered.

"Where do we even start?" Claire asked, her voice filled with a mix of excitement and uncertainty as they browsed the aisles of dusty books.

Lena paused, her fingers brushing against the spines of the volumes, each one a portal to another world. "Let's focus on demonology and folklore," she suggested. "I want to understand who Malphas is, what he can do, and if there's a way to ensure he doesn't come back."

Claire nodded, her eyes lighting up. "Sounds like a plan. Let's split up and see what we can find."

Lena made her way to the mythology section, her heart racing with anticipation. She pulled out several thick tomes, their pages yellowed with age, and settled at a nearby table. The atmosphere buzzed with quiet energy as other patrons drifted in and out, absorbed in their own quests for knowledge. As Lena flipped through the pages of one book, the names of ancient demons and spirits leaped out at her, each entry sending a shiver down her spine. *Malphas—also known as the Grand President of Hell, commanding thirty legions of demons. He appears in the form of a crow or a man, and he can reveal hidden treasures and wisdom... but at a cost.*

Lena's breath hitched as she read on, absorbing every detail. Malphas was not just a shadow; he was a figure of power, steeped in lore and darkness. As she continued her research, Lena learned that Malphas was notorious for manipulating those who sought his wisdom, twisting their desires and leading them astray.

"That's just great," Lena muttered to herself, her thoughts swirling with anxiety. "He wasn't lying when he said he could take my soul."

Across the room, Claire emerged from the folklore section, a pile of books stacked precariously in her arms. "Look what I found!" she announced, plopping down next to Lena. "There's a ton of information about protective symbols and wards against evil spirits."

Lena's eyes widened as Claire opened one of the books, revealing intricate illustrations of symbols—pentagrams, runes, and sigils. "These could be really helpful," Lena said, leaning closer to examine the pages. "If we can find a way to protect ourselves, maybe we can ward off any lingering effects of Malphas."

Claire nodded enthusiastically. "I've also found some rituals for banishing spirits. If we can gather the materials, we might be able to create a protective barrier around your home."

Lena's heart swelled with gratitude. "You're amazing, Claire. I don't know what I would do without you."

Together, they pored over the books, their excitement growing with each discovery. They documented their findings, jotting down notes on protective symbols, rituals, and herbs known for their purifying properties. Time slipped away as they delved deeper into the world of the supernatural, the library transforming into their sanctuary of knowledge.

After hours of research, Lena felt a mix of exhilaration and exhaustion. "I think we've gathered a solid foundation," she said, stretching her arms above her head. "But we need to take action. It's one thing to read about protection, but we need to put it into practice."

Claire grinned, her eyes sparkling with determination. "Let's get the materials we need and set up a protective circle in your room. It'll give you a sense of security."

Lena nodded, feeling a surge of hope. "Yes! I think it's time I reclaim my space."

They left the library, the late afternoon sun casting long shadows on the pavement. Lena's mind buzzed with ideas, her heart racing with anticipation. She couldn't shake the feeling that this was just the beginning of something larger—a journey of discovery, resilience, and empowerment. As they strolled through town, the world around them felt vibrant and alive. The colors of autumn painted the trees in hues of gold and crimson, the air crisp with the promise of change. For the first time in weeks, Lena felt a flicker of joy amidst the lingering darkness. She had taken steps toward reclaiming her life, and that made all the difference. Arriving at Lena's house, they rushed inside, the familiar creaks of the old structure enveloping them like a warm hug.

"First things first," Claire said, rummaging through Lena's drawers for the supplies they needed. "We need salt, candles, and maybe some herbs."

Lena joined in the search, her heart racing with excitement. They gathered everything they could find—a small bowl of salt, white candles for purity, and some sage Claire had brought from her own home. It was a hodgepodge of items, but Lena felt a thrill at the thought of creating a protective barrier.

"Let's do this," Lena declared, setting the materials on her bedroom floor. They drew a large circle with salt, carefully placing the candles at each point of the compass. As Claire lit the candles, their flickering flames danced in the dim light, casting playful shadows on the walls.

"Now we just need to say the incantation," Claire said, flipping through her notes. "This one is supposed to banish any lingering spirits and create a protective barrier."

Lena nodded, her heart pounding in her chest. They stood together in the circle, hands clasped, and as Claire began to recite the words, Lena felt the air around them shift. It was as if the room itself held its breath, waiting for their intentions to take shape. With each word Claire spoke, Lena focused her energy, visualizing a protective light surrounding them. The flickering candle flames danced more energetically, and Lena felt a warmth envelop her, as though the shadows were receding. As Claire finished the incantation, a sudden gust of wind blew through the open window, extinguishing one of the candles. Lena's heart raced as darkness flickered at the edges of her vision, and she exchanged a glance with Claire.

"What was that?" Claire asked, her eyes wide with uncertainty.

"Just a draft," Lena replied, though a knot of fear tightened in her stomach. "Right?"

Claire took a deep breath, her expression steadying. "Let's focus. We finished the incantation. We just need to reinforce the circle."

Lena quickly reached for the remaining candles, relighting the extinguished one as Claire continued to recite their protective mantra. The moment the candle flickered back to life, Lena felt a rush of energy coursing through her, igniting her resolve.

"Malphas may have retreated, but we're not letting him back in," Lena declared, her voice filled with newfound strength.

With each candle flickering brightly, Lena felt the power of their protective circle fortifying around them. The atmosphere shifted, and the shadows seemed to pull away, retreating to the corners of her room, unable to penetrate the sanctuary they had created. As they completed the ritual, Lena and Claire stepped out of the circle, feeling a sense of accomplishment wash over them.

"I think we did it," Claire said, her voice filled with awe. "We actually created a barrier."

Lena smiled, her heart swelling with pride. "It feels different in here. Lighter."

But as they settled back onto the bed, a sudden chill coursed through the room, causing the candle flames to flicker wildly. Lena's stomach dropped as a low whisper echoed in the silence, almost inaudible but unmistakable—words she could not understand. Lena and Claire exchanged startled glances, the weight of the moment crashing down around them. The shadows may have been held at bay for now, but the darkness was far from defeated.

Lena's heart raced as she whispered, "What was that?"

"I don't know," Claire replied, her voice trembling slightly. "But it sounded... angry."

Lena took a deep breath, her resolve hardening. "We'll figure this out. Together."

As they faced the unknown, Lena realized that this journey was just beginning. The shadows may have retreated for now, but she was ready to confront whatever lay ahead. With Claire by her side, she would stand strong against the darkness and uncover the truths hidden within the shadows. They had fought against Malphas, but now they had to face the repercussions of that battle—the echoes of the past that were unwilling to let go. And as Lena steeled herself for the challenges to come, she knew that no matter how daunting the path ahead seemed, she would no longer walk it alone.

Chapter 12

The days that followed the protective ritual were a whirlwind of unease and anticipation. Lena felt an invisible thread tying her to the world of shadows, and every creak of the house made her heart race. Despite the protective circle, a lingering dread loomed over her, whispering reminders of the darkness they had encountered. Lena and Claire decided to meet again at the library, diving deeper into their research about Malphas and the nature of possession. They were determined to uncover the truth behind the doll and its sinister ties to the demonic figure. As they settled at their usual table, Lena laid out the notes they had gathered so far.

"Okay, let's review what we know," Claire suggested, her brow furrowed in concentration. "Malphas is a demon known for manipulation and deceit. He thrives on creating chaos in the lives of those who summon him."

Lena nodded, her fingers tracing the edge of the table. "And the doll… it's not just a vessel for him. It feels like it has its own will, as if Malphas is using it to get to me."

Claire flipped through their notes, her face serious. "We need to understand why he chose you, Lena. There has to be something about you that he wants."

A chill ran down Lena's spine at the thought. "Maybe it's because I'm vulnerable. I've felt lost and disconnected since moving here."

"Or maybe it's because of the grief you've been carrying. Malphas could sense that," Claire added thoughtfully. "Demonic entities often prey on emotional weaknesses."

Lena's heart ached as she recalled the profound loss that had shadowed her life. The absence of her parents, the upheaval of moving to a new town—it was a tapestry of sadness that Malphas might have found irresistible.

"Let's focus on breaking this connection," Lena said, determination surging within her. "I don't want to be a pawn in his game anymore."

The girls spent hours buried in books, unearthing various methods of banishment and protection. They discovered that many cultures had rituals designed to sever ties with malevolent spirits. Some called for offerings, while others required deep meditation and introspection.

"I found this one," Claire said, her finger tapping on a page. "It suggests that we create a 'spirit box'—a place to contain the energy of the entity and prevent it from affecting you."

"A spirit box?" Lena echoed, intrigued. "How does that work?"

"It involves creating a physical container filled with items that symbolize the entity's power. Once it's made, we can perform a ritual to trap Malphas in it," Claire explained. "But we'll need specific items—things that represent the darkness he brings."

"Like the doll," Lena murmured, her heart racing at the thought. "It's been the center of all this. If we can safely contain it, we might be able to weaken Malphas."

Claire nodded, her expression resolute. "Let's get started. We'll need a wooden box, some salt, and personal items that carry your energy—something that represents your past or the things you want to let go of."

They gathered their materials and left the library, the weight of their task pressing down on them. The air outside felt thick with anticipation, and Lena couldn't shake the feeling that they were being watched. When they arrived at Lena's house, the shadows seemed to cling to the walls, as if they were alive, whispering secrets she couldn't quite grasp. She pushed aside her unease and led Claire to her bedroom.

"First, let's create the spirit box," Lena said, her voice steady despite the knot of fear in her stomach.

They found a small wooden box hidden in a corner of Lena's closet, dust covering its surface. As Claire cleaned it, Lena thought about the items they needed to place inside.

"I think I'll add a piece of jewelry from my mom," she said quietly. "Something that connects me to her, but also represents letting go of the grief that's been holding me back."

Claire smiled softly. "That's a great idea. I'll find something personal too."

After rummaging through her things, Claire produced a small locket that had belonged to her grandmother. "This has been in my family for generations. I think it will add some weight to the box," she said, her voice tinged with emotion.

With their items in hand, they carefully placed them inside the wooden box along with a handful of salt—a powerful symbol of purification. Lena felt a wave of resolve wash over her as she closed the lid, sealing the energy within.

"Now we need to perform the ritual," Claire said, her expression serious. "We should light candles around the box to create a sacred space."

As they arranged the candles, Lena felt a growing sense of urgency. "What if this doesn't work? What if Malphas finds a way to escape?"

Claire met her gaze, her eyes filled with determination. "We've come too far to turn back now. We're taking control."

Once everything was set up, they stood in a circle around the box, their hearts pounding in unison. Claire recited the incantation they had chosen, her voice steady and strong. As the words filled the air, Lena focused her energy on the box, visualizing the containment of Malphas within it. The candles flickered violently, casting erratic shadows on the walls, and Lena felt the room shift as if an unseen force was pushing against them. A cold wind blew through the room, extinguishing one of the candles, but Claire didn't falter. She continued reciting the incantation, her voice unwavering. Lena's breath hitched as the shadows around them thickened, coiling like smoke. She glanced at the box, and for a fleeting moment, she thought she saw something shifting inside—a dark presence stirring, eager to break free.

"Keep going!" Lena urged, her voice rising above the growing wind. "Don't stop!"

Claire's voice intensified, and Lena poured every ounce of her will into the ritual. She imagined the box as a prison, its walls fortified against the darkness. With a final flourish of Claire's words, the room erupted in a blinding light, and Lena felt a rush of energy explode outward, pushing back the shadows. As the light dimmed, Lena gasped, feeling an overwhelming weight lift from her shoulders. The air grew still, the shadows retreating to the corners of the room. They had done it.

Claire stepped forward and carefully opened the box, revealing the items inside, now shimmering with a faint light. "It worked!" she exclaimed, her eyes wide with astonishment.

Lena felt a rush of relief, but just as quickly, a chill crept back into the room, making the hairs on the back of her neck stand on end. "Wait... something feels off."

A low rumble echoed in the distance, like thunder rolling across the sky. The atmosphere shifted, and Lena sensed a dark energy rising, thickening the air around them. The box trembled on the floor, and the items inside rattled ominously.

"Lena!" Claire shouted, her voice filled with panic. "What's happening?"

Before Lena could respond, the temperature plummeted, and a dark mist began to seep from the box, curling like tendrils of smoke. In horror, they watched as the mist swirled, taking shape before their eyes.

"No!" Lena cried out, backing away. "We need to close it!"

But it was too late. The shadowy form loomed before them, a twisted version of Malphas, his eyes glowing with malice. The very air vibrated with his anger, and Lena could feel the darkness trying to infiltrate her mind, whispering fears and doubts that twisted like a knife in her heart.

"You think you can trap me?" Malphas snarled, his voice a chilling blend of laughter and fury. "You are merely pawns in a game you cannot hope to win."

Lena's heart raced as she gripped Claire's hand tightly. "We can't let him break us!"

With a surge of adrenaline, Lena and Claire stepped forward, their combined determination igniting the energy in the room. They couldn't let Malphas regain control. They had fought too hard to give in now.

"Together!" Claire shouted, her voice filled with defiance.

Lena closed her eyes, focusing on the protective energy they had built. She envisioned the light surrounding them, pushing back against the darkness. "We reject you, Malphas! You have no power here!"

As they stood united, the shadows writhed in agony, and the dark figure faltered. Lena felt the warmth of their connection amplifying their strength. With one last surge of power, they pushed forward, forcing the darkness back into the box.

The mist screamed, a sound that echoed through the walls, sending vibrations rippling through Lena's body. She clutched Claire's hand tighter, refusing to let go. "We can do this!"

With a final incantation, they slammed the lid shut, sealing Malphas within. The room fell silent, and the oppressive energy dissipated, leaving only a soft glow from the candles.

Gasping for breath, Lena and Claire sank to the floor, their hearts racing in unison. They had faced the darkness and emerged victorious—at least for now.

"We did it," Claire whispered, her voice trembling with emotion. "We trapped him."

"But at what cost?" Lena replied, her heart heavy. "He's still out there, waiting for the moment we let our guard down."

Claire nodded, her expression serious. "We need to remain vigilant. The battle isn't over."

Lena glanced at the box, its surface still shimmering faintly. "We'll find a way to keep him contained. We'll figure this out together."

As they gathered themselves, Lena realized that this experience had forged a bond between them that could withstand even the darkest of forces. They were stronger together, and with their combined courage and determination, they would confront whatever lay ahead.

With renewed resolve, Lena stood, her eyes fixed on the box. "Let's find a way to secure it. We can't let him escape again."

Claire smiled, her spirit unbroken. "We'll figure it out. And together, we'll face whatever comes next."

As the candles flickered gently in the dim light, Lena felt a sense of hope blooming within her—a flicker of light in the shadow of uncertainty. They were not just fighting for their own freedom; they were battling against the darkness that threatened to engulf everything they held dear. And together, they would stand strong.

Chapter 13

The morning light streamed through Lena's window, casting soft shadows across the room. Despite the warmth of the sun, Lena felt a chill settle in her bones, a remnant of the night's harrowing events. She had barely slept, her mind replaying the confrontation with Malphas, the echo of his laughter still haunting her thoughts.

"Lena! Are you awake?" Claire's voice rang out from the kitchen, breaking the heavy silence that enveloped the house.

"Yeah, just give me a minute!" Lena called back, pushing herself off the bed. She rubbed her eyes and took a deep breath, trying to shake off the lingering fear that clung to her.

When she finally made her way to the kitchen, the aroma of pancakes filled the air, momentarily distracting her from her worries. Claire stood at the stove, flipping pancakes with a determined efficiency that Lena admired.

"Good morning! I thought we could use a little comfort food after last night," Claire said, her smile brightening the room.

"Thanks, I really appreciate it," Lena replied, sliding into a chair. "I think we both need it."

As they ate, Claire filled the silence with light chatter about school and upcoming events. Lena listened, grateful for the normalcy, but her mind drifted back to the box containing the malevolent force.

"Do you think we really trapped him?" Lena finally asked, her voice quiet. "What if he's just waiting for us to make a mistake?"

Claire's expression turned serious. "I don't know. But we did everything we could to contain him. The box should hold him for now. We just need to be careful."

"Right," Lena said, taking a deep breath. "I just... I can't shake the feeling that he's not done with us."

After breakfast, they decided to continue their research. They needed to fortify their defenses, especially if Malphas was indeed lurking in the shadows. They returned to the library, pouring over ancient texts and local folklore. Hours passed as they sifted through pages filled with incantations, protective symbols, and tales of those who had faced demonic forces before. The more they read, the more Lena realized how unprepared they were.

"Listen to this," Claire said, her finger tracing a line in a dusty tome. "It says here that Malphas is known to feed on fear and despair. If we allow him to exploit our weaknesses, he could regain his strength."

Lena nodded, feeling the weight of Claire's words. "So we have to stay strong. But how do we do that? It's hard to feel brave when he's still out there."

Claire thought for a moment before responding. "We need to gather allies. People who can help us. If we have a support system, we might stand a better chance against him."

"Who do you have in mind?" Lena asked, intrigued.

Claire hesitated, her brow furrowed in concentration. "I was thinking of Jamie and Sarah. They've both shown an interest in the supernatural before, and I think they'd want to help."

"Okay," Lena agreed, feeling a spark of hope. "The more people we have on our side, the better."

As they finished their research, they crafted a plan to meet Jamie and Sarah that afternoon. Lena's heart raced at the thought of sharing their experiences, of revealing the truth about the doll and the darkness they were facing. When they arrived at the park where they agreed to meet, the sun hung high in the sky, but a cloud of unease settled over Lena. The vibrant green grass and the laughter of children playing seemed a stark contrast to the chaos brewing in her heart.

"There they are," Claire said, pointing to Jamie and Sarah, who were sitting on a bench. Jamie's shaggy hair fluttered in the gentle breeze, while Sarah animatedly waved her hands as she spoke.

"Hey!" Lena called as they approached. "Thanks for meeting us."

"Of course!" Sarah replied, her bright smile infectious. "What's up?"

Lena exchanged glances with Claire before taking a deep breath. "We need to talk to you about something serious."

As they sat down, Lena felt her stomach twist with anxiety. She couldn't help but wonder how Jamie and Sarah would react to their story. Claire took the lead, recounting their experiences with the doll, the initial discovery, and the dark presence of Malphas. Lena watched as their friends' expressions shifted from confusion to disbelief, and finally to concern.

"Wait, so you're saying that doll is possessed by a demon?" Jamie asked, his voice tinged with skepticism.

"Not just any demon—Malphas, a powerful entity," Lena interjected, her heart racing. "And he's been trying to manipulate me."

Sarah's brow knitted in thought. "That's... really intense. Have you guys thought about what you're going to do next?"

"We're trying to figure that out," Claire admitted. "We need to strengthen our defenses and find ways to keep Malphas contained."

Jamie leaned forward, a determined glint in his eye. "I'm in. I can help with whatever you need. Just tell me what to do."

Lena felt a wave of gratitude wash over her. "Thanks, Jamie. It means a lot to have your support."

"What about me?" Sarah chimed in. "I want to help too! This sounds like a wild adventure, and I'm all about it."

Lena smiled, warmth spreading in her chest. "We're glad to have you both on board. The more support we have, the stronger we'll be."

As they began brainstorming ideas for protective rituals and additional research, Lena felt a renewed sense of purpose. They discussed everything from creating wards for their homes to developing strategies for confronting Malphas if he chose to reveal himself again. After hours of planning and sharing ideas, Lena couldn't shake the feeling that something was off. A heaviness lingered in the air, an unspoken tension that made her heart race.

"Hey, do you guys feel that?" Lena asked, glancing around at her friends.

"Feel what?" Claire asked, her eyes narrowed in confusion.

"That sense of... I don't know, impending doom?" Lena replied, her pulse quickening.

Just then, a low rumble echoed through the park, shaking the ground beneath them. The sky darkened as ominous clouds rolled in, blotting out the sun and casting an eerie shadow over the playground.

"Uh, that doesn't look good," Jamie said, squinting at the sky.

Lena's heart raced. "We need to get out of here. Something doesn't feel right."

As they stood to leave, a sudden gust of wind whipped through the park, sending leaves spiraling around them. The atmosphere crackled with energy, and Lena felt a shiver of dread race up her spine.

"Run!" Claire shouted, grabbing Lena's hand as they sprinted toward the park exit. Jamie and Sarah followed close behind, their hearts pounding in unison.

Just as they reached the edge of the park, a deafening crack of thunder reverberated above, and the sky erupted in a torrential downpour. Rain lashed against their skin, soaking them instantly.

"We have to find shelter!" Lena yelled, scanning the area for a nearby building.

They spotted a small café on the corner, its lights flickering ominously. Without hesitation, they dashed inside, shaking off the water like drenched animals.

"Let's find a table," Claire said, her voice barely audible over the storm. They settled into a booth, the warm air inside contrasting sharply with the chaos outside.

"What the hell was that?" Sarah exclaimed, her eyes wide.

Lena felt a knot form in her stomach. "I don't know, but it's like he knows we're trying to fight back."

Jamie leaned closer, his expression serious. "Do you think Malphas can manipulate the weather? Or is this just a coincidence?"

"I don't think anything is a coincidence anymore," Lena replied, her heart racing. "We have to be on guard."

As they sat huddled together, the storm raged outside, mirroring the turmoil brewing within them. The wind howled, and the rain battered the windows, creating an atmosphere thick with unease.

Claire pulled out her phone and began searching for anything related to Malphas and weather manipulation. "There has to be something—maybe a clue that can help us understand what we're dealing with."

Minutes turned into an hour as they scoured the internet, but Lena felt the darkness pressing in on her. It was as if Malphas was reaching through the storm, his influence extending far beyond the physical realm.

Suddenly, Claire gasped, her eyes wide. "I found something! It says here that Malphas can summon storms and create chaos as a way to instill fear in his victims. He feeds on the panic and despair."

"Great," Lena said, her voice laced with frustration. "So he's literally using the storm against us."

"We need to figure out how to counter it," Jamie said, determination in his voice. "If he's drawing power from the storm, we have to find a way to disrupt that."

"Maybe we can create a counter-spell?" Claire suggested. "Something that harnesses positive energy to neutralize his influence."

Lena nodded, feeling a flicker of hope. "Yes! If we can channel our strength, maybe we can turn this storm against him."

As they brainstormed ideas for the counter-spell, the storm raged on outside, the windows rattling under the force of the wind. Lena felt a sense of urgency rising within her—a desperate need to confront the darkness that threatened to engulf them all. The four of them spent hours crafting their plan, merging their unique skills and knowledge to create something powerful. Lena felt a shift within her, a growing strength fueled by the support of her friends. Together, they could stand against the tide of darkness that threatened to consume them. Finally, as the storm began to abate, they stepped outside, the air heavy with the scent of rain-soaked earth. The sky was still overcast, but the worst seemed to have passed.

"Let's do this," Claire said, determination etched on her face. "We have to harness our energy and confront Malphas before he can strike again."

As they stood together, Lena felt a surge of power coursing through her veins—a bond forged in the face of adversity, strengthened by their unwavering resolve. They were no longer just individuals; they were a force to be reckoned with.

"Together," Lena whispered, looking at each of her friends. "We can do this together."

With newfound determination, they set out to confront the darkness that lay ahead, ready to face whatever challenges awaited them. The storm may have passed, but the real battle was just beginning.

Chapter 14

The days that followed were a whirlwind of preparation. Lena, Claire, Jamie, and Sarah worked tirelessly to harness their collective energy and strength. The storm that had rattled them served as a constant reminder of the impending threat they faced. Each evening, they gathered at Lena's house, their makeshift headquarters, poring over texts and practicing the counter-spell they had devised. Lena felt a mix of fear and determination as they approached the night of their confrontation with Malphas. She had come to realize that their bond was the key to their success. Every time they practiced the spell, she could feel their energy intertwining, a powerful force growing stronger with each passing day. On the night of the ritual, the air was thick with anticipation. Lena set up the living room with an array of candles, their flickering flames casting shadows that danced on the walls. The atmosphere felt electric, charged with both anxiety and hope.

"Are you all ready?" Claire asked, her voice steady despite the tremor in her hands.

"More than ever," Jamie replied, adjusting his glasses. "We've got this."

Sarah took a deep breath, her eyes shining with determination. "Let's show Malphas that we're not afraid anymore."

With everyone in place, Lena positioned herself at the center of the room, flanked by her friends. Each held a candle, and they formed a circle, their hands joined in solidarity. Lena closed her eyes and focused, drawing on the energy that pulsed around them.

"On the count of three, we'll start the chant," Lena instructed, her heart racing. "Remember to channel all your positive energy into the spell. We need to counter his darkness."

"Got it," they chorused, their voices a reassuring murmur in the tense atmosphere.

"One... two... three!" Lena declared, and they began to chant in unison, their voices rising and falling like waves crashing against a shore.

The words flowed from their lips, an incantation meant to summon light and protect them from the encroaching darkness. As they spoke, Lena felt an overwhelming warmth envelop her, like a gentle embrace. She could sense their energies merging, a brilliant light radiating from their circle. Suddenly, a gust of wind swept through the room, extinguishing the candles and plunging them into darkness. The air grew heavy, charged with malevolence. Lena's heart pounded as she opened her eyes, and a familiar chilling laughter echoed around them.

"Foolish children," Malphas taunted, his voice a low growl that reverberated through the room. "You think you can defy me?"

Lena's breath caught in her throat as she squinted into the dark, trying to find the source of the voice. "We're not afraid of you, Malphas!" she shouted, summoning her courage. "We're here to stop you!"

The darkness coalesced in the corner of the room, and from it emerged the twisted figure of Malphas, his form shifting like smoke. His eyes glinted with malice, and the very air around him seemed to hum with power.

"Such bravery!" he sneered, stepping closer. "But you are nothing against my might. I feed on your fear, and it delights me."

Lena felt a chill run down her spine, but she stood her ground, glancing at Claire, Jamie, and Sarah, who were equally resolute. "We're stronger together, Malphas. You can't break us."

"Together?" Malphas scoffed. "You are weak. The bond you share is fragile, and I will shatter it!"

With a wave of his hand, the shadows in the room twisted and writhed, reaching out to ensnare them. Lena gasped as dark tendrils wrapped around her wrists, pulling her toward Malphas. She fought against them, her heart pounding.

"Stay focused!" Claire shouted, her voice slicing through the fear. "Channel your energy! We can push him back!"

Lena closed her eyes, visualizing the light that had enveloped them earlier. She reached deep within, drawing on her inner strength, the love and support of her friends. "We are not alone!" she shouted, feeling the warmth of their connection intensify.

The darkness wavered as they began to chant again, their voices ringing out against Malphas's oppressive presence. The tendrils hesitated, flickering like candle flames in a gust of wind.

"NO!" Malphas roared, his form shimmering in rage. "You cannot resist me! I am eternal!"

But as they continued to chant, Lena felt the power within her grow. She could see it now—a glimmer of light pushing through the shadows, illuminating the room. The light swirled around them, growing brighter with every word spoken.

Suddenly, Malphas staggered back, his dark form flickering. "What are you doing?" he hissed, panic creeping into his voice. "You cannot hold me!"

Lena's heart soared as the light expanded, filling the room with warmth and brilliance. "We're breaking your hold!" she yelled, her voice fierce. "You don't own us!"

The light surged, and with it, the shadows recoiled, dissipating like mist in the sunlight. Lena could feel Malphas's rage, a tempest brewing as he struggled against their combined force.

"Do not underestimate me, little girl!" Malphas spat, his eyes narrowing. "You have no idea what I am capable of!"

"Show us!" Lena challenged, her spirit unyielding. "We are not afraid of you!"

In a final surge of energy, they shouted the last line of the incantation together, their voices rising above the chaos. The light erupted, flooding the room, pushing back the darkness with blinding intensity.

Malphas shrieked as the light engulfed him, his form distorting and twisting as he fought against it. "This is not over!" he howled, his voice fading into the brilliant glow.

With a final flash, the light exploded outward, and Lena felt a wave of warmth wash over her. The shadows shattered, retreating into nothingness, and the oppressive atmosphere lifted, leaving only the soft glow of candlelight in its wake.

Breathless and trembling, Lena opened her eyes, the world around her shifting back into focus. They were still in the living room, the candles flickering gently as if nothing had happened.

"Did we... did we do it?" Sarah breathed, her eyes wide with disbelief.

Claire nodded slowly, her expression a mix of relief and exhaustion. "I think we did. I can't feel him anymore."

Lena took a deep breath, her heart still racing. "We fought him back, but he warned us it wasn't over. We have to stay vigilant."

Jamie placed a hand on Lena's shoulder, grounding her. "We'll figure it out. Together."

As they sat in the afterglow of their victory, Lena felt a surge of gratitude for her friends. They had faced the darkness together, their bond stronger than any force that sought to tear them apart. But deep down, a lingering sense of unease remained. Malphas had retreated, but she could sense he would return. The battle was far from over, and they would have to prepare for the storm that lay ahead.

"I think we need to reinforce our protections," Lena said, her voice steady. "We can't let him take us by surprise again."

"Agreed," Claire said, determination gleaming in her eyes. "We'll create more wards, do more research, and strengthen our connection. We've come this far together, and we won't let him win."

Lena felt a spark of hope ignite within her. "And if he comes back, we'll be ready."

As they gathered their resources and began discussing their next steps, Lena couldn't shake the feeling that the true challenge was still to come. But for now, they had prevailed, and together, they would face whatever darkness awaited them.

Chapter 15

The days following the confrontation felt surreal, as if they were stepping out of a nightmare into a world that, while familiar, had transformed. Each of them carried the weight of their battle with Malphas, the experience etched into their minds and hearts. The haunting memory of his chilling laughter echoed in Lena's thoughts, a constant reminder that their victory was temporary. They had managed to push him back, but Lena knew that darkness was persistent, often lurking just beneath the surface, waiting for the slightest crack to exploit. As they regrouped at Lena's house, the atmosphere was thick with uncertainty yet buzzed with an undercurrent of determination.

"Maybe we should consider more aggressive protections," Claire suggested, her brow furrowed as she flipped through a thick tome of spells and wards. "We need something stronger than what we've used so far."

Jamie leaned forward, adjusting his glasses. "What if we could create a barrier? One that he can't penetrate, no matter how much energy he gathers?"

"Or we could look for artifacts," Sarah chimed in, excitement dancing in her eyes. "Things that can amplify our energy or provide additional protection."

Lena listened intently, absorbing their ideas. It was invigorating to see her friends rallying together, each one contributing to the strategy that would fortify their defenses against Malphas. Yet, amid the discussions, Lena couldn't shake the feeling that there was something deeper at play—something tied to the doll that had started this whole nightmare.

"We should also research the doll itself," Lena said, her voice steady. "There must be something in its history that can help us understand what we're dealing with. If Malphas is bound to it, we need to know how to sever that connection."

Claire nodded thoughtfully. "That makes sense. If we can break his link to the doll, it might weaken him significantly."

As they dug deeper into their research, the hours melted away, consumed by books filled with incantations and tales of ancient beings. They scoured the internet for any mention of cursed dolls or artifacts tied to dark forces, scribbling notes and sketching diagrams. Night had settled in, cloaking the house in a shroud of darkness, broken only by the glow of their candles. Lena could feel the weight of exhaustion settling into her bones, but she pushed through, fueled by a mix of fear and determination. They had to act quickly before Malphas could regroup.

"Let's take a break," Jamie suggested, stretching his arms over his head. "We've been at this for hours, and I think we could all use a moment to recharge."

"Agreed," Sarah said, yawning widely. "Maybe we can discuss the next steps over snacks?"

Lena chuckled softly. "You're right. We should celebrate our small victories, too."

As they moved to the kitchen, the tension in the air began to lift. They rummaged through the pantry, pulling out chips and cookies, and as they settled around the table, a sense of normalcy returned—if only for a moment. Laughter bubbled up as they recounted funny moments from their childhoods, their voices lightening the heaviness of their mission. But Lena's mind kept drifting back to the doll. It was a beautiful yet sinister creation, and she couldn't shake the feeling that it was watching them. She had stored it in her room after the confrontation, and every time she glanced at it, a shiver ran down her spine. After they finished snacking, Lena excused herself, needing a moment alone. She climbed the stairs to her room, her heart pounding with a mix of dread and curiosity. The doll sat on her desk, its porcelain face serene yet somehow malevolent in the soft glow of the lamp.

"Why did you choose me?" Lena whispered, her voice barely audible. "What do you want?"

As she stood there, the air around her grew thick, almost electric. A low hum resonated in the room, and she felt an undeniable pull toward the doll, as if it were beckoning her closer. Lena hesitated, torn between fear and an inexplicable urge to understand. She took a step forward, reaching out to touch the cool surface of the doll's cheek. A jolt of energy shot through her, and she gasped, yanking her hand back. Suddenly, the room shifted. Shadows began to creep along the walls, swirling in a dark dance. The doll's eyes glimmered with a life of their own, and Lena's breath quickened. She could feel the presence of Malphas rising within the shadows, his laughter echoing through her mind.

"You thought you could banish me?" he mocked, his voice a low growl that reverberated around her. "You are so naïve."

Lena's heart raced as she fought against the encroaching darkness. "I'm not afraid of you!" she shouted, her voice trembling. "You don't control me!"

But Malphas merely laughed, a chilling sound that sent a shiver down her spine. "You are bound to the doll, Lena. You and your friends are mere pawns in a game far greater than you can comprehend."

"No!" she cried, shaking her head. "We're stronger than you think!"

With a surge of adrenaline, Lena focused on the warmth of her friends, the bond they had forged. She reached deep within, drawing on their collective strength, and channeled it toward the doll. The shadows hesitated, flickering at the edges of her vision.

"Your connection is powerful," Malphas sneered, but there was a hint of uncertainty in his voice. "But it won't save you."

Lena stood her ground, pouring her energy into the doll, determined to break whatever hold it had over her. "I am not your pawn!" she shouted again, feeling the surge of her friends' support in her heart.

With each passing moment, the light within her grew, battling the shadows threatening to engulf her. The room vibrated with energy as she fought to reclaim her power.

"NO!" Malphas roared, and the darkness writhed in protest. "You cannot win!"

But Lena's resolve strengthened. "We will find a way to stop you!"

The light exploded outward, pushing back the shadows and illuminating the room with blinding brilliance. Lena felt the warmth wrap around her like a protective cocoon, and she could see the shadows retreating, their power waning in the face of her determination.

"Together," she whispered, remembering the bond she shared with her friends. In that moment, the connection surged, and she felt their presence beside her, anchoring her against the storm.

The shadows dissipated, retreating into the corners of the room, and with them, Malphas's laughter faded into an echo, leaving a profound silence in its wake. Gasping for breath, Lena collapsed onto her bed, the remnants of energy coursing through her. She stared at the doll, its porcelain surface now seeming more lifeless than before.

"What have I done?" she murmured, the weight of the encounter settling over her. "What does this mean?"

She remained in her room, the silence pressing against her, her mind racing. Lena knew that they had only scratched the surface of the darkness that bound them to Malphas. The battle was far from over, and they needed to uncover the truth behind the doll and its connection to the malevolent force that had haunted them. With renewed determination, Lena climbed out of bed and made her way back downstairs, where her friends were still chatting animatedly, oblivious to the storm that had raged within her.

"We need to meet," she said, her voice firm as she entered the living room. "There's more we have to figure out, and I think it's all tied to the doll."

Claire and Jamie exchanged concerned glances, while Sarah nodded eagerly. "What do you mean?"

"I just had an encounter with Malphas," Lena explained, her heart still racing. "He's tied to the doll, and I think we need to dig deeper into its history to understand how to break his hold."

The mood shifted, tension returning as they realized the gravity of Lena's words. "What do you suggest?" Jamie asked, his voice steady.

Lena took a deep breath, feeling the weight of their collective resolve. "Let's investigate the origins of the doll. If we can learn about its creation and its past, we might find a way to sever the connection to Malphas once and for all."

"Agreed," Claire said, her determination matching Lena's. "We'll research everything we can find. We need to act fast before he comes back for us again."

As they gathered their notes and resources, Lena felt a sense of purpose ignite within her. They had faced darkness together, and now they were ready to confront it once more. The battle was far from over, but together, they would uncover the truth and stand strong against the malevolent force that threatened to tear them apart. In that moment, Lena knew they were not just fighting for their own safety but for something much greater—their bond, their friendship, and their very souls. The doll's sinister grip may have been strong, but they were determined to break free, united in their fight against the encroaching darkness.

Chapter 16

The following days were consumed by research and a relentless pursuit of knowledge. Lena and her friends met daily, their determination palpable as they unearthed every scrap of information they could find about the doll and its sinister history. Their living room transformed into a chaotic hub of books, old photographs, and handwritten notes, each piece a puzzle that needed to be solved. Lena had taken the lead, her mind racing with possibilities. She felt an urgency driving her, a need to understand the nature of the curse that had befallen them. They were bound to the doll, and with each passing day, Lena could sense its hold tightening, its presence lurking in the corners of her mind.

"Okay, I found something," Claire announced one afternoon, her voice cutting through the chatter as she clutched an ancient-looking book. The spine was cracked, and the pages were yellowed, but the title gleamed with a hint of mystery: *Legends of the Cursed Dolls*.

"Let's hear it," Jamie said, leaning forward with curiosity.

Claire flipped the book open, her eyes scanning the text. "Listen to this: 'Cursed dolls often serve as vessels for dark entities, allowing them to manipulate the world of the living. The bond between the doll and its owner can grant the entity power, feeding off the emotions and fears of those around it.'"

Lena's heart raced as she absorbed the words. "So, if Malphas is using the doll to gain power, we have to find a way to break that bond."

"Exactly," Claire continued, her finger tracing the lines of text. "And here's something interesting: 'To sever the connection, one must uncover the doll's origins, its creator, and the intent behind its creation. Only then can the curse be lifted.'"

Lena felt a thrill of hope. "So, if we can find out who made the doll and why, we might have a chance."

Sarah, who had been skimming through old newspapers, suddenly looked up, excitement lighting her eyes. "Guys, look at this!" She held up a brittle article, its edges frayed. The headline read: *Local Artisan Disappears Under Mysterious Circumstances.*

"Let me see that," Jamie said, reaching for the paper. He began reading aloud. "Margaret Waverly, a renowned doll maker, vanished from her home three years ago, leaving behind a collection of her intricate creations. Residents have reported strange occurrences surrounding her workshop, suggesting her dolls may harbor a darker essence."

Lena leaned closer, her heart pounding. "Margaret Waverly. That must be the creator of the doll!"

Claire's eyes sparkled with realization. "If we can find her workshop, maybe there are clues left behind—something that explains the doll's true nature."

"Let's go," Lena urged, the thrill of discovery igniting a sense of adventure within her. "We can't waste any time."

They quickly gathered their things, excitement mixing with anxiety as they prepared to embark on a journey that could uncover the truth behind the doll and Malphas. As they stepped out into the crisp afternoon air, Lena felt a sense of purpose swelling within her. This was the first tangible step toward breaking the curse. The drive to the outskirts of town felt charged with energy, the landscape blurring as they passed familiar streets. Lena's thoughts raced with possibilities. What would they find at the workshop? Would they encounter remnants of Malphas's power? When they finally arrived, the workshop loomed before them—a quaint yet eerie structure hidden beneath a canopy of overgrown trees. Vines snaked up the sides, twisting around the wooden frame as if nature were trying to reclaim it. The windows, once bright, were now clouded with dust, shrouding the interior in shadows.

"Do you think anyone's been here since she disappeared?" Sarah asked, her voice barely above a whisper as they stepped out of the car.

"Only one way to find out," Lena replied, her heart racing as they approached the door.

It creaked ominously as they pushed it open, revealing a dimly lit interior filled with the scent of aged wood and varnish. Shelves lined the walls, stacked high with unfinished dolls and various crafting materials, each one appearing eerily lifelike. Lena shivered, a sense of foreboding washing over her.

"Stay close," Jamie murmured, his eyes darting around the room as they stepped inside.

Lena led the way, her pulse quickening as they ventured further into the workshop. Dust motes danced in the air, illuminated by slivers of light streaming through the grimy windows. A sense of history hung heavy in the atmosphere, and Lena could feel the weight of the past pressing down on them. In one corner of the room, a large worktable was cluttered with tools, fragments of fabric, and half-finished dolls. Lena approached it cautiously, her fingers brushing against a doll that seemed to stare back at her with unsettling eyes.

"This place feels... off," Claire whispered, glancing at the dolls surrounding them. "Like they're all watching us."

"Maybe they are," Lena replied, her voice barely a whisper. "We need to find something—anything—that will help us understand what happened here."

As they searched, Lena's heart raced with anticipation. She rummaged through drawers filled with sketches and notes, each piece providing a glimpse into Margaret Waverly's mind. But nothing seemed to reveal the truth they sought.

Then, Sarah's excited gasp drew their attention. "Look at this!" She held up a small, ornate box, its surface covered in intricate carvings. "It looks like it's been here a while."

"Open it," Jamie urged, his curiosity piqued.

With trembling hands, Sarah lifted the lid, revealing a collection of delicate trinkets—miniature charms, thread, and a small, beautifully crafted doll that looked remarkably like the one Lena had at home.

"This is... beautiful," Claire breathed, reaching out to touch the doll. But as her fingers brushed against it, a chill raced through the room. The atmosphere shifted, growing thick and oppressive.

"Did you feel that?" Lena asked, her heart pounding.

"Yes," Claire replied, her expression turning serious. "It's like something just changed."

Lena's pulse quickened as she peered closer at the small doll. "What if this is a prototype? It looks just like the one I have."

Suddenly, the lights flickered, and a low rumble echoed through the workshop, making the ground tremble beneath them. The shelves rattled, and dust fell from the ceiling, landing on their shoulders like remnants of the past awakening.

"Get back!" Lena shouted, grabbing her friends and pulling them away from the table. They stumbled backward as the energy in the room surged, dark shadows swirling around them.

Malphas's voice filled the air, cold and mocking. "You seek answers, but you cannot comprehend the truth!"

"Show yourself!" Lena demanded, her heart racing as the shadows coalesced into a dark figure, flickering and shifting.

"Margaret Waverly was no ordinary doll maker," Malphas hissed, his form becoming clearer. "She sought to imbue her creations with life, to grant them souls. In her desperation, she made a deal with me—one that sealed her fate."

"What did you do to her?" Lena shouted, feeling the energy swell within her.

"I granted her wish, but it came at a price," Malphas sneered. "She became a vessel for darkness, just as your precious doll is now. Her spirit is trapped within, feeding my power."

Lena felt a wave of nausea wash over her as realization dawned. "You used her! You took her soul!"

"Her essence is mine to command," Malphas replied, the shadows around him writhing like snakes. "And now, you are bound to her fate as well. You cannot escape."

"No!" Lena shouted, shaking with rage. "We will find a way to free her! You won't win!"

As the darkness surged toward them, Lena felt her friends rally around her, their energy combining into a powerful force. They had faced Malphas before, and they wouldn't back down now.

"Together!" Lena yelled, raising her arms as they focused their energy on the darkness. "We can push him back!"

The light within them flared, illuminating the shadows with brilliant warmth. The air crackled with energy as they fought against the encroaching darkness. Malphas shrieked in frustration, his form flickering as the light pushed him back.

"Foolish children!" he roared. "You cannot comprehend the power you meddle with!"

But Lena felt a surge of confidence. "We will break this curse! We will free Margaret and ourselves!"

With a final surge of energy, they channeled their combined strength into the light, driving it forward like a spear piercing through the darkness. The shadows screamed as they were engulfed, and Malphas's form disintegrated into a whirlwind of smoke. As the darkness receded, Lena's heart raced with exhilaration. They had pushed him back again, but the fight was far from over. Breathless, they gathered their strength, the echoes of Malphas's laughter still ringing in their ears. Lena turned to her friends, their faces illuminated by the fading light.

"We have to find a way to free Margaret," she said, her voice steady despite the fear coursing through her veins. "We have to understand what we're dealing with if we want to break the curse."

"Agreed," Claire said, determination etched on her

face. "Let's search the workshop for more clues. There has to be something here that can help us."

As they resumed their search, Lena felt a flicker of hope. They were not alone in this fight. Together, they could uncover the truth and confront the darkness that threatened to consume them all.

Chapter 17

The tension in the workshop hung thick in the air as Lena and her friends continued their frantic search for clues. Dust motes swirled in the dim light, illuminated by the fading sun streaming through the grimy windows. The shadows had receded, but the chill of Malphas's presence lingered, a reminder of the battle they had just fought. Lena moved to a large bookshelf laden with books and journals, the spines cracked and faded with age. She ran her fingers across the titles, searching for anything that might shed light on Margaret Waverly's life and her twisted creations. "There has to be something here," she muttered, pulling a book from the shelf and flipping it open. The pages were filled with sketches of dolls, each one more intricate than the last.

"Lena, look at this!" Jamie called from across the room, his voice echoing with excitement. He stood by the worktable, holding a dusty old ledger, its cover cracked and worn.

"What did you find?" she asked, hurrying over to join him.

"I think this is Margaret's work log," Jamie said, his brow furrowing as he flipped through the pages. "It details her projects and the materials she used, but there are also notes about her experiments." He paused, glancing at Lena. "She wrote about trying to infuse her dolls with life. Look at this!"

Lena leaned in closer, her heart racing as she read the entry aloud. "March 15, 2017: I've discovered a technique for animating my dolls.

It requires rare materials and a deep connection to the spirit world. I must be cautious; the energy I'm tapping into is volatile."

"What does she mean by 'volatile'?" Claire asked, her eyes wide with concern.

Jamie continued reading, his voice low. "I feel a presence guiding me. It whispers secrets and dark promises. I must tread carefully, but the allure of bringing my creations to life is too strong to resist."

Lena exchanged worried glances with her friends. "This is it. This is how she made the deal with Malphas."

"Look at this one," Sarah said, pointing to another entry. "It's dated a week before she disappeared. 'I've made a breakthrough. The doll's eyes—when they are complete, they will be the key to its soul. I can feel the energy coursing through me.'"

Lena felt a cold shiver run down her spine. "The eyes... they're the connection. We have to figure out what she meant. If we can understand how she infused the doll with life, we might find a way to reverse it."

"Wait, there's more," Jamie said, flipping to a page filled with strange symbols and sketches. "These look like rituals or sigils. Maybe they're linked to the binding process."

"Let's take pictures of everything," Lena suggested, pulling out her phone. "We need to document this."

As Lena snapped photos, she could feel the weight of the workshop pressing down on her. Each sketch, each entry, felt like a thread weaving a darker tapestry of Margaret's descent into madness. It was clear that her obsession had drawn her into a dangerous world, one where she had willingly surrendered herself to Malphas.

"Look at this!" Claire exclaimed, pointing to a folded piece of paper tucked between the pages of the ledger. "It looks like a letter."

Jamie carefully unfolded the paper, revealing a hastily scrawled note. "Margaret, I cannot continue this path. The whispers grow louder, and the dolls... they are changing. I fear I've lost control."

Lena felt her stomach drop. "This must be from one of her friends or family. It sounds like they were worried about her."

"'If you don't stop this madness, you will regret it. I'm coming to see you,'" Jamie read aloud, his voice trailing off. "This doesn't sound like a letter of support."

"Do you think they went to see her?" Claire asked, her voice laced with concern.

"Maybe they were trying to save her," Lena said, contemplating the implications. "But what happened? Did they come too late?"

As they pieced together the fragments of Margaret's life, Lena felt an overwhelming urge to understand the woman behind the cursed doll. She was more than just a creator of nightmares; she was a person who had lost her way in the pursuit of her art.

"Let's search the workshop for more clues," Lena suggested, feeling invigorated by their discoveries. "There has to be something that explains her connection to Malphas."

They split up, each taking a different area of the workshop. Lena returned to the shelves, her eyes scanning the titles of dusty books. One caught her eye—*The Art of Doll Making: Techniques and Traditions*. She pulled it off the shelf and flipped through the pages, finding illustrations of dolls from various cultures, some with alarming features and unsettling histories.

"Lena!" Claire's voice broke through her thoughts. Lena turned to see her friend standing near the worktable, excitement dancing in her eyes. "You have to see this!"

Lena rushed over, her heart racing as she found Claire holding an old photo album. "What did you find?"

Claire flipped through the pages, revealing faded photographs of dolls and their creators. "Look! There's Margaret with her dolls. She looks so happy."

Lena studied the images, noting the intricate designs of the dolls and the pride in Margaret's expression. But as they flipped to the next page, Lena's breath hitched in her throat. The next photograph was dark and disturbing—a doll with hollow eyes and a twisted smile, its arms outstretched as if beckoning for attention. Behind it stood Margaret, her expression one of manic joy, but her eyes—those were filled with something unsettling, something dark.

"Is that the doll?" Sarah whispered, peering over Claire's shoulder.

"Yeah," Lena replied, her heart pounding. "It looks just like mine."

"Do you think it's... possessed?" Claire asked, her voice trembling.

"I think it's more than that. It looks like the doll had a life of its own," Lena replied, her mind racing. "This was no ordinary doll maker."

As they continued flipping through the album, Lena's unease grew. The further they went, the more the dolls transformed. The last pages were filled with eerie photographs of Margaret working on the dolls, her once-joyful demeanor replaced by an obsessive focus, her eyes wild with fervor.

"Look at her hands," Jamie pointed out, noticing the faint traces of dark ink smeared on Margaret's fingers. "It's almost as if she was drawing something onto them."

"What if she was?" Lena suggested. "What if those symbols are linked to the ritual she performed?"

"Let's check the other side of the workshop," Claire said, her voice urgent. "There might be more information there."

They moved to the opposite wall, where an array of tools and supplies hung in disarray. As Lena rummaged through a drawer, her fingers brushed against something cold and metallic. She pulled out an ornate box, much like the one they had found earlier, but this one was larger and intricately carved.

"What's that?" Jamie asked, eyeing the box with curiosity.

"I don't know," Lena replied, running her fingers over the carvings. "It looks like it has symbols on it."

As she opened the box, a rush of stale air escaped, and inside, they found a collection of strange items—twisted metal charms, bits of thread, and a small mirror. The mirror was cracked, and Lena felt a wave of unease wash over her as she looked at her reflection, the edges warping her image.

"What do you think these are for?" Sarah asked, peering over Lena's shoulder.

"I think they might be part of the rituals," Lena replied, her heart racing. "We need to take everything we can. If any of this is linked to the doll, it could help us break the curse."

"Let's gather everything," Claire suggested, her voice steady despite the tension that filled the air.

As they collected their findings, Lena's mind raced with questions. How had Margaret's obsession driven her to this point? What darkness had she unleashed upon the world? As they prepared to leave the workshop, Lena paused, her gaze lingering on the photos lining the walls. In one final moment, she felt a pull, a whisper from the past urging her to remember Margaret not just as a cursed doll maker but as a woman who had sought to create beauty and connection.

"Let's go," Lena finally said, her voice resolute. "We have the information we need, but we're not done yet. We have to confront Malphas and find a way to free Margaret."

As they stepped out of the workshop and into the fading light, Lena felt a sense of determination ignite within her. They had faced the darkness before, and they would do so again. Together, they would uncover the truth and confront the evil that sought to claim them.

Chapter 18

The night deepened as Lena and her friends made their way back to Jamie's house, their arms laden with the evidence they had unearthed. The atmosphere outside was thick with foreboding, the moon a ghostly orb hovering in a sea of clouds. The chill in the air sent shivers down Lena's spine, a harbinger of the darkness they were about to face. Once inside, the group gathered in Jamie's dimly lit living room, their findings sprawled across the coffee table like pieces of a puzzle waiting to be solved. The old ledger, the photographs, the ornate box—each item pulsed with a sense of urgency. Lena's heart raced as she studied the collection, aware that they were at a precipice, standing on the edge of something ancient and malevolent.

"Okay, we need a plan," Lena said, her voice steady despite the unease gnawing at her gut. "We've gathered enough information to confront Malphas, but we have to be careful. We don't know what he's capable of."

Jamie nodded, his brow furrowed. "We've seen what he can do. The attacks, the whispers... it's all connected to Margaret and the doll. If we're going to end this, we need to be united."

"Agreed," Claire added, her expression serious. "We've already faced him once, but next time, we'll be ready. We have to use the rituals Margaret wrote about."

Lena picked up the work log, her fingers tracing over the notes about the rituals. "These sigils... they have to be the key. If we can replicate her methods, we might be able to summon Malphas and bind him back to the doll. But it won't be easy. We need to be prepared for whatever he throws at us."

"Let's practice the rituals first," Sarah suggested, her voice laced with determination. "We should know what we're doing before we confront him."

As the group set to work, they divided the tasks. Jamie meticulously documented the sigils from Margaret's log, while Claire and Sarah began gathering materials—a candle, a bowl of salt, and various herbs that would be used in the rituals. Lena took the lead in preparing the space, dimming the lights and clearing a central area for their gathering. The energy in the room shifted as they worked, an electric charge that tingled against Lena's skin. It felt as if the very walls were alive, holding their breath as they prepared to face the unknown. She could feel the weight of the doll's presence lingering in the background, a shadow that refused to fade. As they arranged their makeshift altar, Lena felt a rush of doubt. What if they failed? What if Malphas was too strong? She pushed the thoughts aside, focusing on the task at hand. They needed to do this for Margaret, to free her from the dark bond that tethered her to the doll.

"Alright," Lena said, gathering everyone's attention. "Let's start with the first ritual. This one is meant to strengthen our connection and prepare us for what's to come."

The group formed a circle around the altar, their hands joined together. Lena lit the candle, its flickering flame casting long shadows across the room. She closed her eyes, drawing in a deep breath, centering herself.

"Spirits of the night, we call upon you," she began, her voice firm yet reverent. "We seek guidance and strength in our quest to confront the darkness that plagues us. We are united, and we ask for your protection."

As Lena spoke, she felt the air around them thicken, the atmosphere charged with anticipation. The flame danced wildly, and a faint whisper, almost inaudible, echoed through the room. The hairs on the back of her neck stood on end, and she opened her eyes to see Jamie's face pale with shock.

"Did you hear that?" he whispered, his voice trembling.

Lena nodded, heart racing. "It's just the energy... we're tapping into something."

"Let's keep going," Claire urged, squeezing Lena's hand. "We can do this."

They continued with the rituals, each incantation growing more intense. Lena guided them through the sigils, tracing them in the air with her fingers, their meanings swirling in her mind. The darkness seemed to respond, a palpable force that slithered around them, testing their resolve. As they chanted, the candle flickered violently, and a low rumble echoed from the shadows. Lena's heart pounded in her chest as she sensed Malphas's presence drawing nearer, a dark cloud coalescing in the corner of the room.

"Stay strong," Lena urged, her voice rising above the chaos. "We're not afraid of you!"

In response, the temperature plummeted, a gust of icy wind sweeping through the room. The candle sputtered and nearly extinguished, casting them into near darkness. Lena squeezed her eyes shut, focusing on the warmth of her friends' hands in hers.

"Keep chanting!" she cried, urging them on. "We have to hold the circle!"

With each incantation, Lena felt a flicker of power building among them. The shadows writhed and twisted, forming shapes that clawed at the edges of her vision. She could hear the whispers, incoherent yet haunting, as if the darkness itself was alive, mocking their efforts. Suddenly, the whispers coalesced into a voice, deep and resonant, echoing with malice.

"You think you can stop me? You are nothing but mere children playing with forces beyond your understanding."

The voice sent a jolt of fear through Lena, but she forced herself to respond, her voice steady. "We're not afraid of you, Malphas! You've taken enough from us!"

Laughter erupted from the shadows, dark and sinister. "Fear is the least of your concerns, child. You meddle with things you cannot comprehend. I am eternal; I thrive on your fear and desperation."

Lena felt a surge of anger rise within her, fueling her determination. "You're wrong. We know the truth now, and we're going to end this!"

As they continued their chant, the darkness began to swirl violently, the shadows closing in on them. Lena felt a pull, as if Malphas was trying to draw them into his abyss. "Hold tight!" she shouted, her voice echoing with urgency. In that moment, Lena reached deep within herself, recalling the images of the dolls, of Margaret, of all the pain that Malphas had inflicted. She envisioned the sigils glowing with light, the power of their united will pushing back against the darkness.

"By the power of the light, we bind you!" Lena shouted, her voice resonating with authority. "You have no hold over us!"

The shadows writhed in protest, but Lena felt the strength of her friends surrounding her, their determination solidifying their resolve. As they continued to chant, the candle flickered back to life, a beacon piercing through the encroaching darkness.

"Lena!" Jamie shouted, his eyes wide with fear. "Look!"

Lena turned her gaze towards the corner where the darkness coiled, and her breath caught in her throat. From the shadows emerged a figure, tall and imposing, its form cloaked in a shroud of darkness. Malphas stood before them, his eyes glowing like embers, filled with malice and fury.

"You think you can banish me?" he hissed, his voice a low rumble. "You are mere mortals, fragile and weak!"

With a surge of adrenaline, Lena stepped forward, refusing to back down. "We are not afraid of you! You've taken Margaret's life, but we're here to set her free!"

Malphas laughed, a deep, mocking sound that reverberated through the room. "You are brave, but foolish. Your spirit is admirable, but you cannot defeat me. I am bound to this doll, and I will not be released!"

Lena clenched her fists, feeling the energy within her swell. "We are stronger together, Malphas! We will break your hold!"

As the darkness coiled around Malphas, Lena felt the sigils glowing brighter, their power resonating through her. She raised her hands, channeling that energy into a brilliant beam of light that surged toward the dark figure.

"No!" Malphas shouted, his form flickering as the light hit him. "You cannot... you will not..."

Lena's friends rallied beside her, their voices rising in unison, a chorus of determination echoing through the room. Together, they pushed back against the darkness, the light illuminating every corner of the space, banishing the shadows that sought to engulf them. With a final surge of strength, Lena unleashed the full power of their combined will. The light erupted, filling the room with a blinding radiance that shattered the darkness.

As the brilliance engulfed Malphas, his screams filled the air, a cacophony of rage and despair. "You cannot hold me! I will return!"

With a final flash, the light consumed him, and then silence fell. The shadows dissipated, the oppressive atmosphere lifted, leaving only the warm glow of the candle illuminating the room.

Lena stood trembling, the adrenaline still coursing through her veins. She looked at her friends, their faces pale but resolute. "Did we do it?" she whispered, the weight of their victory settling over them.

"I think... we did," Jamie replied, his voice shaky but filled with wonder.

Claire's eyes widened as she scanned the room. "But what about the doll?

Is it over?"

Lena felt a mixture of hope and trepidation as she turned to the doll sitting silently on the worktable, its eyes staring blankly ahead. "We need to make sure."

They approached the doll cautiously, each step filled with uncertainty. Lena reached out, her fingers brushing against the cool porcelain. She could feel a shift in the energy surrounding it, a residual tension that hinted at the struggle they had just faced.

"Lena?" Sarah said, her voice barely a whisper. "Do you think it's really over?"

"I don't know," Lena admitted, her heart racing as she examined the doll. "But we need to try."

With a deep breath, Lena focused on the sigils from Margaret's journal, recalling the words of the ritual. "Together, let's bind the energy," she said, her voice steady. "We can free Margaret and put an end to this once and for all."

As they gathered around the doll, they formed a circle, their hands clasped tightly. Lena led them in the chant, feeling the power surge once more, wrapping around them like a protective cocoon. As they repeated the incantation, Lena felt the energy of the room shift, the air vibrating with anticipation. The doll's eyes glimmered for a moment, and Lena held her breath, hoping against hope that they were finally breaking the curse. With each repetition of the chant, the light grew brighter, illuminating the room and casting long shadows on the walls. The doll began to tremble slightly, the porcelain surface vibrating with the force of their combined will.

"Come on!" Jamie urged, his voice rising in fervor. "We can do this!"

As they chanted, the light enveloped the doll, wrapping it in a cocoon of energy. Lena felt a connection to Margaret, a whisper of her spirit urging them on. "We're here for you," she called, her voice strong and steady. "We will set you free!"

The light blazed, a beacon of hope piercing through the darkness. With one final surge, the energy coalesced, binding the doll and releasing the lingering remnants of Malphas's hold. And then, silence. Lena opened her eyes, breathless and trembling. The air was still, and the oppressive weight that had filled the room was gone. The doll sat quietly, its eyes no longer glowing, but the darkness within it had lifted.

"Did it work?" Claire whispered, her voice filled with disbelief.

Lena took a step back, her heart racing. "I think so," she breathed. "I think we did it."

As they stood together, the reality of their victory began to sink in. They had faced the darkness and emerged stronger, united in their determination to protect each other and break the curse.

"Let's get some rest," Jamie suggested, a smile breaking across his face. "We've earned it."

But even as they left the room, Lena felt a flicker of unease within her. Though they had faced Malphas and fought against the darkness, she knew that the battle wasn't truly over. The scars of their encounter would linger, and the memories of their struggles would remain etched in their hearts.

"Tomorrow, we'll figure out what to do next," Lena said, glancing back at the doll one last time. "But tonight, we celebrate our victory."

As they headed upstairs, laughter and relief echoed through the house, a stark contrast to the darkness that had threatened to consume them. Lena felt a warmth spread within her, a sense of accomplishment and camaraderie that reminded her of the strength they had found in each other. But deep down, she couldn't shake the feeling that Malphas's whispers still lingered in the shadows, waiting for an opportunity to rise again.

Chapter 19

The morning light filtered through the curtains, casting a warm glow across Jamie's bedroom. Lena awoke to the sound of laughter drifting up from the living room, the remnants of last night's confrontation still fresh in her mind. She sat up slowly, the events of the previous night playing like a vivid dream. Had they truly faced Malphas and banished him? The thought sent a thrill through her, but also a lingering sense of dread. With a deep breath, she swung her legs over the side of the bed and stood, shaking off the remnants of sleep. The soft carpet cushioned her feet, grounding her as she moved toward the door. The laughter grew louder, mixed with the sound of clinking dishes. Jamie and Claire must be in the kitchen preparing breakfast. As she stepped into the hallway, a sense of camaraderie filled the air, pushing back against the shadows that still clung to her thoughts. She could hear snippets of conversation—Sarah's laughter, Jamie teasing Claire about her cooking skills, the lighthearted banter weaving a comforting tapestry around her. Lena made her way down the stairs, her heart lighter with each step. The smell of pancakes wafted through the air, rich and inviting, stirring her stomach into action. As she reached the bottom, she paused to take in the scene. The kitchen was a whirlwind of activity, with Jamie flipping pancakes while Claire set the table. Sarah was perched on a stool, scrolling through her phone and giggling at something that made Jamie roll his eyes dramatically.

"Good morning, sleepyhead!" Claire called out, her voice bright and cheerful. "Hope you're ready to eat; we've got enough food here to feed an army!"

"Or at least a group of tired teenagers," Lena replied, joining them at the counter. She grabbed a plate as Jamie slid a stack of pancakes her way.

As they gathered around the table, the warmth of the morning enveloped them, momentarily dispelling the lingering shadows from the night before. They chatted and laughed, sharing stories and teasing one another, allowing the comfort of friendship to wrap around them like a warm blanket. But beneath the surface, a tension simmered. Lena could feel it in the way Jamie occasionally glanced at the doll, now sitting quietly in the corner of the living room, its once-ominous presence diminished but not entirely gone. They had faced Malphas, but had they truly rid themselves of his influence?

"Hey, has anyone checked on the doll since we finished?" Lena asked, her voice cutting through the lighthearted chatter. The room fell silent, eyes shifting towards the doll as if it were a living thing.

"Not since last night," Claire admitted, her brow furrowing. "Do you think it's... safe?"

"I don't know," Lena replied, her heart quickening. "But I think we should keep an eye on it. Just in case."

Jamie sighed, setting down his fork. "I don't want to sound paranoid, but maybe we should do another ritual. Just to make sure everything is really okay."

Lena nodded, grateful that Jamie understood her concerns. "That makes sense. We need to reaffirm our bond and protect ourselves."

"I can help gather the supplies," Sarah offered, her enthusiasm cutting through the lingering unease. "We can even make it more of a celebration, you know? Like a cleansing ceremony."

"Good idea," Claire said, a hint of relief creeping back into her voice. "Let's make it something positive. We'll banish any lingering darkness and celebrate our victory over Malphas."

As they finished breakfast, the atmosphere lightened again, laughter echoing through the house. They cleared the table, each taking turns washing dishes, the rhythmic sound of water blending with their chatter. The camaraderie was palpable, a bond forged through shared trials and the determination to stand against darkness. After the dishes were done, they gathered in the living room, eyes drawn to the doll that had once been a vessel of horror. Lena approached it cautiously, her heart pounding. She felt the weight of their previous encounters pressing against her, the memory of Malphas's wrath echoing in her mind.

"Let's do this," she said, trying to sound braver than she felt. The others joined her, forming a circle around the doll. Lena pulled Margaret's journal from her bag, the pages worn and filled with hope and despair, a testament to their struggle.

With the candle set before them, Lena opened the journal to the page with the cleansing ritual. "We need to remember why we're doing this," she said, looking into the eyes of her friends. "We're here to protect each other and to ensure that Margaret is finally at peace."

Jamie nodded, determination etched on his face. "Let's bring in all the good energy we can. We've already faced the worst; we can't let it creep back in."

Lena took a deep breath, focusing on the candle's flickering flame. She lit the sage and let the smoke rise, filling the room with its earthy scent. "We call upon the spirits of light to guide us and protect us. We stand united against the darkness."

As they chanted together, Lena felt the energy shift in the room. The candle flickered brightly, casting shadows that danced across the walls, and for a moment, Lena felt a sense of peace wash over her. They were in this together, their bond stronger than any darkness. But just as the warmth enveloped them, a sudden chill swept through the room, sending shivers down Lena's spine. The smoke from the sage twisted violently, spiraling towards the ceiling as if pulled by an unseen force. Lena's heart raced; the familiar weight of dread pressed against her chest.

"Did you feel that?" Claire asked, her voice barely above a whisper.

"Yeah," Lena replied, her breath quickening. "Something's not right."

Suddenly, the doll's eyes flickered with an eerie glow, the porcelain surface shimmering with an unsettling light. The room plunged into an unnatural darkness, the warmth of the candlelight snuffed out as shadows enveloped them.

"Stay together!" Jamie shouted, but his voice was swallowed by the encroaching darkness. The shadows writhed, twisting around them like a living entity, threatening to pull them apart.

Lena's heart raced as she held tightly to Claire's hand, her voice steady despite the panic rising within her. "We have to keep chanting! We can't let it take us!"

"Spirits of light, we call upon you!" they chanted, their voices echoing in the suffocating darkness. But the shadows pressed in harder, whispering, taunting, filling the air with promises of despair.

"You thought you could banish me so easily?" a deep voice echoed, reverberating through the room. "I am eternal, bound to this world by your fear!"

Lena felt the icy grip of dread around her heart, but she refused to yield. "We are not afraid of you, Malphas! You will not take us!"

"Foolish mortals," he sneered, the shadows pulsing with malevolence. "You have only delayed the inevitable. I will always return!"

In that moment, Lena closed her eyes, envisioning the light that had engulfed Malphas during their last confrontation. She could still feel the flicker of hope within her, a spark that refused to be extinguished. "Focus on the light!" she urged, her voice rising above the chaos. "We can do this together!"

As the darkness roiled around them, they clung to each other, chanting louder, each repetition of the incantation bolstering their resolve. Lena felt the energy within her surging, a fierce determination igniting her spirit. She envisioned the doll, its form flickering, the darkness within struggling against the light.

With one final push, Lena opened her eyes and shouted, "By the power of our friendship, we bind you once more! You will not take hold of us again!"

The candle flared back to life, illuminating the room with a blinding light. The shadows shrieked in protest, recoiling as the warmth washed over them. Lena felt the bonds of darkness shattering, the whispers fading into silence.

The light enveloped Malphas, his form distorting and flickering as the energy surged around him. "No! This cannot be!" he howled, his voice filled with rage and despair.

But Lena felt the weight lifting, the chains of fear breaking as they chanted with renewed strength. The shadows dissipated, retreating into the corners of the room, and the light expanded, filling every crevice with warmth and love. With a final surge of energy, they pushed back against the darkness, the light surging forward to engulf Malphas completely. The room erupted with brilliance, illuminating the doll, which now shimmered with a newfound light. As the darkness faded, silence filled the space, leaving behind a sense of peace that settled over them like a soft blanket. Lena collapsed onto the floor, breathless, her heart pounding with the remnants of their battle.

"Did we do it?" Jamie gasped, his eyes wide with disbelief.

Lena glanced around, her heart still racing. The shadows had retreated, and the air felt lighter, free of the oppressive weight that had burdened them for so long. "I think... we did," she replied, a smile breaking across her face.

Claire knelt beside the doll, reaching out to touch its cool surface. "It feels different," she said, awe in her voice. "It's like... it's been cleansed."

Lena felt a wave of relief wash over her. They had faced the darkness once more and emerged victorious, but as she looked at the doll, she couldn't shake the feeling that their battle was not entirely over. The remnants of Malphas's darkness still echoed in her mind, a reminder of the struggle they had faced.

"Let's take a moment," she suggested, feeling the exhaustion creep in. "We've been through so much."

They sat together in a circle around the doll, the light from the candle illuminating their faces as they shared their thoughts. Lena reflected on the strength of their bond, how it had pulled them through the darkest moments. As they talked, the sun began to set outside, casting a golden hue across the room. The shadows receded, replaced by the warm glow of twilight. Lena felt a sense of hope beginning to blossom within her, a belief that they could overcome anything together. But as the night deepened, a flicker of doubt lingered at the edges of her thoughts. What if Malphas returned again? What if the darkness found a new way to infiltrate their lives?

"Lena?" Jamie's voice broke through her reverie. "Are you okay?"

She nodded, forcing a smile. "Yeah, just thinking."

"About Malphas?" Claire asked, her brow furrowing with concern.

"More like... what comes next," Lena admitted. "We need to stay vigilant. We can't let our guard down, not now."

"We'll face it together," Jamie reassured her, his gaze steady. "We've already proven that we're stronger than we thought."

Lena felt a warmth spread within her, the bond they shared a fortress against the darkness. They would stand united, ready to confront whatever came their way. But as she glanced at the doll, a flicker of uncertainty remained, a whisper that reminded her that the echoes of the past were never truly gone.

Chapter 20

The soft glow of dawn filtered through the windows, bathing the room in a warm, golden light. Lena sat on the floor, the remnants of the previous night's ritual still lingering in the air. The doll rested quietly nearby, its presence now feeling more like a guardian than a threat. The weight of fear had lifted, replaced by a sense of hope and renewal. As the first rays of sunlight crept into the room, Lena felt a wave of peace wash over her. They had faced darkness and emerged victorious, their bonds stronger than ever. But even in the tranquility of the morning, a part of her remained vigilant, aware that the shadows could return. Lena's thoughts drifted back to their confrontation with Malphas, the chilling whispers and the overwhelming darkness that had threatened to consume them. But in that moment of terror, they had found strength in each other. She smiled at the memory of their united voices, chanting against the evil that sought to tear them apart. The sound of footsteps echoed from the hallway, pulling Lena from her reverie. Claire appeared, her hair tousled and eyes still heavy with sleep. "Good morning," she yawned, stretching her arms above her head.

"What time is it?"

"Almost sunrise," Lena replied, glancing at the clock on the wall. "I thought I'd take a moment to gather my thoughts."

Claire plopped down beside her, her expression shifting from sleepiness to curiosity. "About what happened last night?"

Lena nodded, taking a deep breath. "Yeah. I just keep thinking about how close we came to losing everything. It's hard to shake off that feeling."

"I know what you mean," Claire said, her brow furrowing. "But we're still here. We made it through, and we're stronger for it."

"Stronger together," Lena echoed, feeling the warmth of their friendship envelop her like a protective shield. "I think we should write down everything that happened, maybe even document our rituals. Just in case."

Claire's eyes sparkled with enthusiasm. "That's a great idea! It can be like our own little journal of experiences. Plus, if anyone else ever finds themselves in a situation like ours, they'll have a guide."

"I love that," Lena replied, feeling a flicker of excitement. "We can include everything—the rituals, what worked, what didn't. It'll be a record of our journey."

As they spoke, the others began to emerge from their rooms, drawn by the smell of freshly brewed coffee that Lena had set to percolate earlier. Jamie was the first to join them, tousled and bleary-eyed, followed closely by Sarah, who was still adjusting her glasses.

"Morning, everyone!" Jamie greeted, rubbing his eyes. "What's the plan for today?"

"Claire and I were just talking about documenting everything that happened," Lena explained. "We want to make sure we remember what we did to confront Malphas and how we overcame it."

"Sounds like a great idea," Sarah said, her voice brightening. "We could even create a scrapbook! Something visual to remember all of this by."

Lena smiled, grateful for their enthusiasm. "Exactly! It'll be a project we can all work on together. A way to keep the memories alive."

As they settled into a comfortable rhythm, the atmosphere in the room shifted from one of lingering tension to a vibrant energy filled with laughter and creativity. They gathered supplies, pulling out colored paper, markers, and the remnants of the sage they had used in their rituals.

"Let's start with the rituals we performed," Jamie suggested, flipping through Margaret's journal. "We can illustrate them and add notes about what we felt during each one."

They spent the morning reliving their experiences, crafting pages filled with sketches, notes, and thoughts. Each word written and every image drawn seemed to solidify their bond, reinforcing the idea that they had triumphed together. Hours slipped by, and the sun climbed higher in the sky, filling the house with light. The laughter and chatter flowed freely as they worked, their shared energy creating an atmosphere of celebration. Finally, they took a break, flopping onto the living room floor, exhausted but fulfilled. Lena leaned back against the couch, her heart swelling with gratitude for the friendship they had forged. "We did it," she said softly, glancing around at her friends. "We faced darkness and came out stronger. We're a team."

"Always," Jamie agreed, grinning. "And if anything ever happens again, we'll be ready for it. Together."

As they sat in comfortable silence, Lena's thoughts drifted to the doll. It had been the catalyst for their struggles, the source of fear and darkness. But now it seemed like a silent witness to their journey, a reminder of the strength they had found.

"What do you think we should do with the doll?" Claire asked, breaking the silence and bringing Lena back to the moment.

Lena considered the question, feeling a sense of responsibility. "Maybe we should keep it, but in a safe place. We can't forget the lessons we learned, and having it around could serve as a reminder."

"I agree," Sarah said, nodding thoughtfully. "It can be a symbol of our victory over fear."

They decided to find a special place for the doll, somewhere that honored its journey while also signifying their triumph. They chose a shelf in the living room, placing it among photos of their memories together—happy moments, adventures, and laughter. The doll now seemed like part of their story rather than just a vessel of darkness. As they stepped back to admire their work, Lena felt a sense of closure wash over her. They had faced fear, darkness, and uncertainty, and yet they had emerged stronger than before. The scars of their experiences would always remain, but they would not define them.

"Hey, let's make a pact," Jamie said suddenly, his eyes sparkling. "No matter what happens in the future, we stick together. We're stronger united, and we'll always have each other's backs."

Lena's heart swelled at his words, the sincerity in his voice echoing the strength of their bond. "I agree," she said, reaching out to clasp his hand. "Forever."

"Forever," Claire and Sarah echoed, their hands joining the circle.

As they stood together, Lena felt a sense of hope blooming within her, a belief that they could face anything that life threw their way. They had each other, and that was the most powerful weapon against the darkness. The day passed, filled with laughter and creativity, as they transformed their experiences into a tangible record of their journey. They promised to revisit the journal often, to remind themselves of the strength they had found together. As night fell and the stars twinkled above, Lena reflected on how far they had come. The shadows of the past had not vanished completely, but they no longer held the same power over her. The warmth of friendship and the lessons learned would carry them through whatever challenges lay ahead. As she looked at the doll, now resting peacefully among their cherished memories, Lena knew that she was ready to embrace whatever came next, with her friends by her side.

About the Author

I have been wanting to write books for a while but never knew how. When writing a book, I always go with something random and don't always know what I want to write about. Sometimes there are a lot of different reasons for this, but for me personally, I just think of something random and go with it. There are times when I will use an AI to help me, but I was just messing around. I love how this book turned out and I hope you enjoy it.

Milton Keynes UK
Ingram Content Group UK Ltd.
UKHW021119021124
450589UK00014B/1229